The
SECRET
WINDOW

A story of a remarkable journey

from darkness into light

Oliver Drake

Published by Quest Partners, Adelaide

www.questcounsellingskills.com.au

Email: quest@adam.com.au

First printed June 2018

ISBN 978-0-9587692-6-6

A catalogue record for this book is available from the National Library of Australia

Contents

Foreword

This book is an interesting, easy to read adventure story set in several countries - Norway, Spain, Peru, Brazil – as it tells the story of the spiritual journey of the hero as he lives through a wide range of experiences. It is, in part, science fantasy!

The writing is sometimes harsh and crude – and sometimes gentle and poetic. It is also occasionally reminiscent of Dickens! It vividly describes the harsh life on a commercial fishing boat and it sensitively describes the amazing and beautiful spiritual capacities of Peruvian shamans.

At the start of the story, Alexander is earning extremely good wages by fishing commercially in the North Sea. The ship's crew is a collection of societal misfits who manage their dysfunctional personalities with a mixture of violence, booze and drug use. Alexander is no exception. When the ship finally docks with its catch, Alexander and a ship colleague have abundant money to go travelling. After an alcoholic, drug-taking binge, they are totally surprised to find themselves having chartered a plane to Brazil.

This is the start of a remarkable journey for Alexander as he drifts through many experiences, with different kinds of people. Some of the people he meets are as vicious as the ones he is familiar with, but others inhabit secret worlds he has never known. Alexander's journey – and his response- could inspire your own journey.

Read it!! It may well form the basis of the next big popular sci-fi movie.

Vicky Sanders PhD

1. Anger

It was the same as always. It was the same as it always has been. It was the same every time. Some people would stand and some people would sit, all of them drinking. They moved from the bar to the dance floor. Their eyes are searching the room. Everyone is looking for someone.

They are looking for someone who is looking for them: for someone to connect with. They are looking for someone whose puzzle is seeking their piece, for someone to give them the space to be what they otherwise couldn't. These people are exploring themselves, their inner selves. They are exploring themselves through others, and they do not even know they are doing it. How blind can they be?

I took a long drink.

It was the same music that played. It was the same music that always played. The same music that had played for the last month while I was fishing at sea. I looked around the room and back to my drink. It does not get much more stupid than this. Such painful music. So loud. Such people. So mindless. All of them are made in the same factory and pressed from the same mould. Every time I come to land it is the same. They wear the same clothes and they walk the same way. They have the same mind, and they strut in this bar the same way they parade the streets—with the belief they are better than others. With bigger muscle and a more expensive dress, they believe they are better than others. They are better than others because of their car. They are better than others because of their house. They are better than others because of their clothes, their money and the way they look.

How stupid can people become?

I finished my drink and ordered another, then glanced around the room and back to my drink. There are those that want to fight you, and there are those that want to take you home and cook you breakfast. I watch as the beer from their glasses pours into their mouths. They are a plague to this world and everything is going according to their plan. They are a plague that is normal. As normal as this world is normal. As normal as fish is meat. As normal as its life means nothing. No one will question that a fish is worth less than a man.

But fish don't produce enough junk products to fill the ocean. And fish don't stick signs on every corner, advertising the junk they have produced, signs that fill the eyes of these mindless people with hypnotic colours, as they fill this bar with their empty chatter. They drink and dance happily to poisonous music. Mindless people. They are worth nothing—no more than a fish. I drink from a bottle. I will not touch a glass that they use. I exhaled and let my drink sit on the bar. Time off the ship—away from the weather and the long days at sea. Time for a good drink—to forget about fish and the constant bad weather we had sailed through.

The ship's engineer had walked off with a woman, and I sat, ignoring people's chatter and the painful music that surrounded me. I looked at no one, my eyes to the bar in front, looking at nothing, drinking my bottles of beer. Just me and my bottles of beer, and the bartender who gave me another every time I emptied.

I leaned my stool back from the bar as I dug through my pockets, searching for any thing I might have. Balancing my stool on its back wooden legs, hoping to find something to lift my mood. There was nothing. Nothing but a small square of hash and a packet of prescription pills.

Change.

Like a needle pushing that delightfully evil heroin into your blood, it only takes a moment for everything to change. A push of junk or a handful of pills and everything changes, like death or sudden loss when everything is gone. It can be the loss of something good or it can be the loss of something bad. Change can happen in a moment. It can happen slowly, and you can see it as it happens, you can prepare for it and there is no shock. However, change can happen quickly, and there is shock. There is a shock because what was the same is different. This is something I knew, that change could happen in a moment.

I proceeded to pop each pill from its foil casing when I was hit. I was hit with a glass of beer and a fist to the back of my head. The wooden barstool crashed underneath me and I hit the floor hard, landing on broken glass that pushed forcefully into my skin. The floor was wet with beer, and my blood began to mix with it.

I stood up.

Beer saturated my shirt and a piece of glass stuck from my arm. I pulled it out. The cut was deep, and blood ran quickly down the sleeve of my shirt—my attention fixing on several sensations.

I felt the gash in my arm showing different layers of fat and muscle and I felt the blood soaking into the fabric of my shirt. I felt the beer running further past my waist, soaking my groin. Discomfort spread across my face, as I stood staring at this group of men.

They spoke with their eyes and they spoke with the way they stood. We are going to break you into pieces—that is what they said. They were familiar. I had met them before, but I could not remember where. I suspected it was here and that I had been drinking.

Blood continued to soak the fabric of my shirt and alarm bells went off in the room. Alarm bells sounded through the people in the bar and they surrounded me. A circle of people chattering like the thousands of birds that surround the fishing boat. Blood is a shock for them, blood that flows through every one of us, for they have seen nothing of life, so they are alarmed. They are alarmed and they chatter. Chattering that I need help and that I should sit down, chattering because everyone else is, all of them chattering the same. And these men standing before me, they were responsible for the blood and the beer that covered me.

They stood staring. They were ready to move and have me back to the floor. Beer soaked my shirt, pants and underwear. I looked at the blood soaking my clothes while feeling the throbbing in my arm. I looked at these men. These fucking people.

This was a moment of change and there's no turning back. But there's no shock. There is no shock because this is normal. It is as normal as the bar is normal. It is as normal as the music that plays is normal. It is as normal as fish are food and as normal as trees are wood.

A storm. I knew it well. A storm of black, blacker than the dark red blood on the floor. A storm of heat, throbbing in every part of me. Throbbing my eyes and throbbing my ears. Black heat. Black and hot and boiling. There is nothing else. No sound, no thoughts, only red-hot throbbing. Nothing but black heat blocking all sound and all thought. I stared at them.

I wanted their blood to cover the floor. I wanted their bones to crack. I wanted to see the pain it brings them. I wanted them to scream. I wanted to rip their throats from their necks and watch them fall to the ground. I wanted to squeeze and pull their throats, tear them from their necks and stop these fucking people from standing.

Not one of them spoke. The four of them stood there ready to move. 'Four against one,' I said, 'make it a fair fight.' I took a step forward and threw the glass I had pulled from my arm to their feet. 'Bring more,' I said. 'Bring more and make it fair'.

I moved fast and grabbed two of them, each by the shirt of their chest, and slammed one hard to the bar. I felt his teeth break as he fell limp to the ground. I threw the other over the bar, smashing him into the fridges. The glass doors cracked, bottles smashed and the circle of people surrounding me scattered. The circle around me broke and people ran. I grabbed another and slammed his head into the stonewall making a deafening cracking sound, then stepped towards the last of this group and took him firmly by his throat. My hand gripped tightly around his throat. I began to squeeze. I looked into his eyes and I squeezed. I squeezed hard. Tighter and tighter. I held him tight and felt that at any moment his throat would crack. I squeezed, looking into his helpless eyes waiting for his throat to break. Waiting for the crack. Waiting for the life to flow out of him.

It was loud and it was hard.

Crack!

So very hard. I lost balance and stumbled to the ground, falling to one knee. Black and silver stars passed through everything. Black and silver throbbing in my mind. I couldn't tell where my mind was and where it was not. A moment passed, the stars dissipated and I found my mind. I felt where I was, but black, still black. Wow, such a good hit. I was dazed, I could not focus, and I simply prepared myself for another blow. Nothing but black, as I ran my hand over my head, fearing I had been struck with a bottle.

The black faded and my world came back into view and it was not a bottle, it was the engineer and he was holding his fist, which must have been sore, for he had hit me hard.

He came properly into focus and a smile came over my face. He must have hit me by mistake, assuming I was one of them. I was happy to see him and impressed at the punch he delivered. I stared at the engineer, who stood staring at me holding his fist. I looked around the room. It was empty and I reached over the bar and took a bottle. The engineer slapped it from my hand, smashing it to the floor.

'For Christ sake!' the engineer yelled, 'you gonna kill everyone?'

The engineer's eyes drove heavily into mine. I stared at him.

'Goddamn drink Alexander! Come on,' he said, 'lets get the hell out of here!' I looked around the bar. Things were broken and men lay still on the floor.

We hopped over the bar, walked through the kitchen, and exited through the back door that led to a side street. We moved staying in the shadows, and avoided passing cars until we were down by the water where we stopped and sat.

The engineer pulled out a ball of hash and rolled a joint. 'What the hell do you think Alexander?' he asked.

I said nothing.

Russ handed me the burning joint and we talked. Mostly Russ talked and mostly I listened. I thought about the month ahead of me. I looked at the cut in my arm. It was deep and blood stained my clothes. I opened and closed my fists; pleased I had not damaged them, as I would be working with my hands for the following month. I looked from the water to Russ and my hands shook with the thought, as the remainder of the dead joint fell to the cement.

'You think those men are alright?' I asked.

Russ just looked at me.

'You wanna hope so,' he said.

2. The usual day

I woke up to the noise of the engine pushing the ship through the water.

The curtains to my window were open and I saw we were still in the fjords. It was dark, but the moon was bright and it lit up the mountains that lined the fjords. A small gill-net fishing boat passed by, the size for just a few men. I was happy the ship had left the dock. I was happy to be away from the men that lay in that bar.

I had seen it before—the Norwegian coast—the same fjords we had sailed through countless times on our way to the open ocean. The red houses that lined them and the many vessels that sailed through them. We were heading north and moving at full speed, to the Arctic, close to Russia, where at this time of year was our fishing ground.

I stepped into my bathroom and drank directly from the faucet, rubbing my eyes, feeling my heart thump still pushing alcohol through my blood. My head was sore and I needed to clean my arm. I focused to the mirror and opened my mouth. I had all my teeth, just the usual gap between the front two.

I closed the door to my cabin while exhaling a breath, then walked to the mess.

Breakfast was the same everyday. It had been the same everyday since I first put a foot on this ship, and I didn't believe it was going to change. There was always eggs. Eggs for breakfast was a sure thing, as was sleeping at night. And bacon, there was always bacon. Bacon in oil and, if you felt like it, there was about ten types of boxed cereal. Today the cook had boiled the eggs, so I took an eggcup and sat down—my hands trembled as I took off the top of my egg with my spoon.

 We spent the day preparing line and doing what was needed to get the ship ready for when we arrived at the fishing ground. Life at sea is routine and it is always the same.

We were deep-sea long-line fishing, where line the thickness of your small finger lies on the bottom of the ocean. Attached to this line at every metre is a hook. A hook with bait. The line is weighted to the bottom with anchors at each end, preventing the line from moving with the currents, and line running from the anchors to the surface is attached to floating buoys and a flag. Coordinates are marked where the line is situated, and the ship is free to move and set as many lines as it has anchors and buoys.

We fixed some new line and threw away that which was getting too old. I checked we had everything ready and that everything was in working shape, and the day ended as it always did. Everything ran as it always had. Fishing was fishing and everything was the same.

Everyday dinner was always the same, for the cook had a list of meals and he stuck by them. Some people knew what was for dinner because they knew what day of the week it was. I knew what day of the week it was when I saw what was on the table.

Today was roasted pork and boiled potatoes. Today was Monday. The cook was always good and I always ate until I was full. There are no surprises on the ship, and surprises that do occur are predictable anyway, so they are no surprise.

After I eat I turn on the sauna. A small element heating a small room, it is my time to unwind after a days work.

I opened the hatch to the stern of the ship and walked the steps to the top deck. It was winter and it was cold and snow fell almost horizontally as the ship steamed ahead. I found a spot away from the large amounts of garbage that was the remains from unpacking food and bait, which cluttered the deck and I sat, letting the air and snow move through my skin and into my bones. Real cold, when you feel it in your bones. Cold that hurts.

I sat until my skin was ice and my flesh was frozen. I sat until my bones were as cold as the hard steel deck. Until I shivered. It does not feel good to be cold, but it feels good to be in the sauna after you have been.

The sauna was small and could tightly fit three, but I was the only one who used it so I always had it to myself. I let the heat from this small room warm my skin and sink into my bones. I sank comfortably into the wooden bench of the sauna, and soon sweat was dripping from every piece of my skin. Toxins from my body coming out. I poured a bucket of water over my head and washed away the sweat, then turned off the element.

I made a joint, and fell easily into a good after-sauna sleep.

Back on the ship. The only home that I knew.

The Secret Window

3. The good and the bad

I woke to the sound of the bait machine.

Click, click, click, click, click, as the blade of the automatic machine cut a piece of squid, and one of the thirty thousand hooks pulled through it and fell into the ocean—we were setting the line in the water. I put my slippers on, walked to the galley and poured some coffee. I looked at the date on the TV—I had slept for a full day.

I wanted to sleep more. I rolled a cigarette.

Apart from the cook preparing lunch, the galley was empty. I lit my cigarette and looked at the work schedule on the table.

Twenty-four hours in a day means nothing here, we work on our own clock. Sometimes we work twelve hours on with four hours rest. Sometimes we work eight hours on with eight hours rest. It depends on how many crew are aboard and how much fish we are catching. The ship is always running, it is always fishing, and we are always working.

I would be on shift after lunch and work with a new man who had just finished school. It was more work to train someone new, but I had done so before. I had done this job for so many years, I could close my eyes and do the same as always.

I had met this young man the previous day and I liked him. He was quick to learn and worked hard. I took a drink from my coffee.

The aroma of fresh bread the cook had made wafted from the kitchen, it filled the galley and moved through the halls of the ship. I inhaled deeply this delicious smell as Vegor, the young man I would be on shift with, walked into the mess. He gestured a small hello with his eyes as he walked past, then collected some coffee and sat across from me on the sofa facing the TV.

I pointed at the roster on the table.

'You are working with me,' I said, 'and we go on shift after lunch'.

Vegor turned from the TV to me and I was about to explain to him the process of the day when Dimitri, a man who had worked on this ship as long as I had entered the galley. He turned to Vegor.

'Are you serious?' Dimitri asked Vegor.

Dimitri held his finger to the young man's face, his voice was rising and his lips were beginning to tremble. He looked as though he was a shaken fizzy drink and his lid was about to be opened. He looked as though he might cut the throat of the new man right here.

Vegor said nothing and I sipped my coffee ignoring Dimitri for he was often angry. Unlike myself, he did not need a head full of booze for his anger to fill the room.

'Three days,' Dimitri yelled, 'are you serious?' 'You have been on the ship for three days, when I tell you to do something you do it!'

He stuck his finger closer almost touching the new man's face. Dimitri was shaking.

'If that deck is not clear from garbage and I have to do it, I will throw you over with it!' he yelled, then stormed out the galley mumbling as he went, 'useless good for nothing damn kids.'

Dimitri was not a tall man, but he was large and he was strong, and I had seen men three times his size back away from his temper. I knew his temper and although I had not been on the receiving end of it, I had seen what it was capable of. I had seen him lost in his temper, and his temper when lost is ferocious. Unlikely he would cut the throat of another man at sea—perhaps I thought, he could learn from the trouble this has previously caused him.

I leaned into the comfortable leather of the sofa.

This is where they come.

The outcasts from society, the ones who don't fit in on land. They go to sea and the ships are full of them. What land does not tolerate lives on the water. Anger and violence lives here, and it is ok. It is normal and normal is whatever it is that happens.

I smiled and pushed my pouch of tobacco toward Vegor who rolled and lit a cigarette.

'Don't worry about him,' I said, 'but do what he says, he's alright when things are running smoothly.'

Vegor looked at me as if I was as mad as Dimitri.

'He told me to throw the garbage into the sea,' Vegor explained. 'It's in plastic bags. He told me to throw garbage and plastic to the sea. I'm supposed to throw that to the ocean?' Vegor asked.

He looked at me and I looked at Vegor.

'It's a big salty ocean,' I said, 'we don't live down there. 'Come on,' I said as I punched him gently in the arm and smiled. 'We have to keep the ship clean and we don't need rubbish laying around when there's work to be done'.

Vegor looked into his coffee.

'Go on,' I said, 'clean that mess up. Then we will eat, and then we will see if we have any fish'.

The ship slowed down and I heard the anchor hit the side of the hull on its way to the bottom of the ocean as Vegor left his half drunk coffee and walked out.

The crew had finished casting the line and like clockwork the cook was setting the table with a selection of sliced meats, pickled fish, cheese and bread. He set a pot of boiled potatoes on the warming station, along with boiled carrots, boiled cabbage and brown sauce to accompany the pork.

The crew that had been working casting the line came and sat around the table. I rolled another cigarette, waiting for them to finish, before taking food. Vegor came back in and sat down. He looked troubled. I watched as Dimitri scraped the leftovers from his plate to the rubbish. Not a trace of trouble was about Dimitri, and as he walked past where we sat he did not look at nor say a word to Vegor.

I ate a large helping of meat and potatoes, and as usual I ate until I was full. I felt fat and I was glad we had a little time before beginning to haul the line in. Time for my stomach to settle and time to explain to Vegor what we would be doing and what he didn't know.

I was surprised Vegor had a good understanding of the ship. He questioned me about weather, the currents, and the machinery. He asked where equipment was stored and what to do in certain situations. I liked his clear mind, I liked his focus and I liked that he listened to me. I had seen already the previous day he knew a few knots and that he could mend line—it seemed he would be an easy person to train.

The skipper spoke over the intercom, saying in his usual calm manner that we would arrive at the buoy in ten minutes.

'Come,' I said to Vegor, 'we shall start to pull the line.'

We changed into our weather clothes and I took a knife and a couple of gaffs forward then opened the large hydraulic bulkhead. The ship was still moving fast, and in the distance I could see the orange buoys and flag covered with reflector tape.

It was cold and I hoped there would be fish on the line, as there is nothing worse than just standing feeling cold. The ship slowed down and drifted past the buoys and flag. I threw the grappling hook between the flag and buoy, caught the line and pulled them in.

I wrapped the line around the block, a type of pulley the line goes around, which grips the line and pulls it in from the water. We were fishing deep, and after the block pulls in the line that connects the floating buoys to the anchor it meets the line with baited hooks— and fish.

I explained to Vegor, as I showed him, to wrap the line around the block and tie it to another line that moves through to the back of the ship, where whoever is on shift would mend the line, change damaged hooks and prepare it to be cast out again.

Vegor took the buoys and flag to where we stored them and I waited for the anchor to come up.

I explained to Vegor you could tell when the anchor came loose from the ocean bed, as the tension in the line would loosen. I turned to Vegor.

'Watch for the anchor,' I said. 'Don't roll a cigarette now and don't play with your music. If you don't pay attention, if you don't stop the line when the anchor comes up, it will come hurling over the side of the ship and destroy everything in its path.'

I pointed to the space that the line moves through in front of the block. It is big enough for the line to pass through but not big enough for a fish. The block pulls the line through this tight space, but the fish will not fit and the hook attached to the line will pull free from the fish's mouth and the fish will fall into the bin in front of you. Vegor was attentive as I explained.

'If you do not stop the anchor and it comes over the side of the ship, the block will pull the anchor with huge force into this,' I said pointing at the tight space the lined moves through. 'The anchor will destroy this and the engineer will have to fix it and the skipper will be cursing you for time wasted. Not to mention,' I said, 'I have seen the anchor knock a man black, and he had to be collected by helicopter. 'So,' and I told him again, 'watch for the anchor.'

I stopped the block, pulled the anchor aboard, unclipped it from the line and ran the block at normal speed. Vegor picked up the forty-kilo anchor and walked off.

Fish!

Big fish.

Big codfish every hook. The skipper blew his horn and spoke over the intercom.

'Look at the size of them!' The skipper said.

I smiled and Vegor watched. I had not seen fishing like this in a long time. I brought the fish aboard.

It is a simple operation—the block inside the ship pulls the line out of the water and onto the ship and as the fish come out of the ocean, the hook supporting it carries more weight as it leaves the buoyancy of the water and the fish can fall off the hook at this point. So I stand with a gaff—a piece of wood with a sharp steel spike on one end—and stick the fish in the head, and bring them aboard. If a fish falls off and is floating in the water, there is a long pole beside me, with sharp hooks on one end for retrieving it. As the fish come aboard, I cut their throats and throw them to a tank of water. A tank they will sit in for a short time, allowing the blood to run out of the meat. Another man will take off the head and clean out the stomach and put them in the freezer.

I brought the fish on and killed them, and threw them to the tank of water. Good money, I thought—big fish is good money. Big fish sell for the highest price, and they were all big.

After some time cutting so many fish my knife became dull, so I slowed the line down, took the steel next to me and gave my knife a quick sharpen. I sped the line back up and cut the throat of another fish, the blade gliding effortlessly through its neck and the blood came running out.

We were in the Arctic Circle and in the winter the sun does not shine here, and we would not see it again until much later, when returning south to offload our catch. Darkness is the winter and now, with a big moon lighting up a calm sea, I found moments. Moments between the constant flow of fish to rest my eyes on the green and pink lights of the north. The Aurora Borealis. Long waves of smoky green coloured clouds swept the sky. Blotches of pink. Pink and green lights.

These were the good days.

The cold winter air, cooling down the sweat the work produced, and big fish. Keep fishing this good, I thought, keep fishing this good and we will be home early—only three hundred tonne to go.

These were the good days.

The calm weather, the northern lights, the big moon and big fish. I threw another fish to the tank. It was getting full. There was so much fish that the men who were cutting them could not keep up. I threw another fish to the tank.

The tank of water the fish were bleeding in was about to overflow, and still every hook was a huge fish. I could see the buoy and flag, which meant we were coming to the end of the line, and as the line with hooks met the line connected to the anchor I threw down my gaff and let out a breath. I was dripping with sweat, and if I had known the fishing was to be like this, I would not have worn a sweater under my raincoat.

A few remaining fish sat in the box before me, their scales shining as they gasped for life they could not get.

'Cut those fish,' I said, motioning for Vegor to cut the throats of the remaining fish and throw them in the tank.

Vegor picked up the knife and looked at the fish—he just stood there.

I looked at him.

'Cut the fish,' I said, 'we need to finish and get ready for casting this line out again.'

I turned back to wait for the anchor. I stopped the line, unclipped the anchor and Vegor carried it away. I looked down to see the fish still in front of me. I sped up the block, letting it bring in the buoys and flag, then I cut and threw the remaining fish to the tank.

We finished and got the lines, buoys and anchors ready for casting. There is no time wasted. No sooner had we pulled the line in, we were throwing it out again. I rolled a cigarette and watched the line run through the bait machine—click, click, click, click, click.

Dimitri walked behind me.

Good, I thought—shift change. I looked at my watch, he was early and his smile was big.

'Good fishing,' he said.

'Yes,' I said, 'very good.'

Once a week the cook prepared whale meat, which is enjoyed by almost all aboard. It was always served the same way, with boiled potatoes and brown sauce.

With a full stomach, I leaned into one of the comfortable reclining leather sofa chairs, and felt my muscles relax. It had been a strenuous shift and I half paid attention to the news on the large TV. I rolled a cigarette and closed my eyes to the noise of eating, talking and the news presenters.

'Can I take one from you?'

I looked over at Vegor.

He looked tired—his mind looked tired. I understood for he was young, just from school and he was learning the ship. He was learning fishing and we were hit with a huge amount of fish. I knew what Vegor was going through for years ago I had been in his shoes.

'You don't have tobacco?' I asked.

He looked as though he had thoroughly messed up—to come to sea with no tobacco—this was an excellent mistake. I motioned to my pouch.

'Take it,' I said. 'I will leave more in your cabin.'

I pushed myself from the sofa and left the mess.

I switched the element in the sauna on then went to my cabin. I closed the door and looked at the small piece of hash I had remaining, a piece but the size of my thumb. I rolled a joint and took two beers and left them outside in a pile of snow. I had more than enough tobacco and left enough in Vegor's cabin for while he was at sea.

I did what I always did—I read the news on my computer while I waited for the beers to be cold and the sauna to be hot.

It is a good ship, and with Internet, satellite radio and a sauna being off shift was good and is my relaxing time to myself. I walked, towel around my waist to the sauna with two frosted beers and a joint and stood in the shower connected to the sauna. I could feel the sauna was hot, as heat filled the shower area I stood in and the smell of timber hung to this heat. I filled a bucket with cold water and dropped one beer in. I opened the other and took a long drink. I lit my joint, and carrying a bucket in one hand, a beer in the other and a burning joint in my mouth, I kicked the wooden door to the sauna open.

'Vegor?' I said with surprise.

The sauna was hot and Vegor sat in it. A smile stretched across his face as he looked at the burning joint in my mouth and the beer in my hand. I put the bucket down, the beer bobbing as I looked at him. Vegor laughed, and I was glad to see he had no problem with the smoke that was going to fill this small room.

I feel good when I smoke. I handed Vegor the other of my beers and we sat, sweating and sharing the joint I had made.

'I don't have much,' I said, 'just a small square left,' a frown of disappointment sinking over my face.

'Thanks for the tobacco,' Vegor said.

'No problem, I have plenty, I said.'

'You better stay on Dimitri's good side,' I said.

Vegor looked at me.

'I don't like throwing that junk to the sea,' he said.

'I don't like this job,' he said.

I looked at him and I understood, for he was new and things could be tough when you were new. However, he had a strange smile, and I realised I did not understand him. I stared as he took another draw of my joint and I watched it burn down to the paper filter, as what was left was now gone. He blew out, filling the room a little more with smoke.

'I hate throwing trash to the sea,' he said, 'and I hate killing fish.'

Vegor turned to me.

'I watched you do it all afternoon, cut, cut, cut, I watched the blood run out from them all. I don't like killing things,' he said. 'Fish after fish, as they leave the ocean they live in.'

Vegor looked at the joint in his hand, it was finished and he continued talking.

'They come out of the sea, breathing for oxygen they can't find, their eyes looking at the strange place they have just entered, unable to swim in the air of the ship. I don't like this job,' Vegor said again.

He did not search my eyes for response; he did not care; he said what he felt like.

'I didn't cut those fish you told me to cut today,' Vegor said, 'I didn't want to kill them. I believe I have chosen the wrong profession,' he said. Then he chuckled to himself as if it were funny.

I just looked at him.

I looked at the dead joint in his hand. The small amount of hash that I had left had passed through this kid. This kid, who had signed his way aboard a ship, that caught, killed, and froze fish, and he cared about them like they were his pet cat!

I looked at the empty beer can beside him, the beer that I had just given him. I shared with him what little hash I had, and I had given him tobacco for his entire five weeks at sea, and to top if I would have to work with this kid.

A kid who wouldn't even kill fish!

Vegor looked at the paper filter in his hand.

'I'll go make another,' he said.

I stared at him. I watched as he left the room I was just about to throw him out of. Just when I was about to throw him out of the sauna and let Dimitri cut his throat, I suddenly felt a change in mood.

He has hash!

I suddenly felt better about sharing my beer and tobacco.

Vegor came back to the sauna with a huge joint, and it was the best quality hash found in Norway, soft black and sticky. We smoked until we could see nothing in the room and we laughed at how smoky it was. Good hash and a big joint, my muscles relaxed into the heat of the sauna. The sweat poured out and I closed my eyes.

I recalled the look on Vegor's face when he had to throw the garbage overboard. I opened my eyes and took a long draw of his joint. So nicely rolled, perfect, as if machined rolled and sold in the cafes of Amsterdam.

'Why you care about fish?' I asked Vegor.

I looked at him and chuckled. He looked extraordinarily comfortable as if the hard wooden bench in the sauna were as soft as a beanbag. He looked as though he might melt and slide through the spaces between the timbers.

He moved closer towards me, so I could see his face through the smoke. 'They have eyes!' he said, opening his eyes wide, giving me a visual understanding of what eyes were, a big smile stretched across his face as he did. 'Eyes, just like us,' he said. 'They are born, they live and they see, so why should I take its life as if it was nothing?' He leaned back into the wood and closed his eyes and after a moment he said, 'I wonder what it's like to be a fish?'

I looked at Vegor's smiling face as he melted into the wooden bench of the sauna. I poured the bucket of water over my head.

'It's a fish Vegor. It's a damn fish.'

I stood up.

'I'm sure it's a big day tomorrow,' I said, 'so prepare yourself to kill a lot of them,' and before closing the door to the sauna I turned to him.

'We are on a fishing boat, we are people, we are on a ship and they are fish. They are just goddamn fish!'

Vegor did not smile, as he leaned forward and turned off the element.

I went to my cabin and opened another beer. Every time I am at sea it is the same. I always think to spare the beers I have and space them out over the weeks at sea. However, every time I open one I finish them all. I took a long drink from the can and placed it on my table. I swallowed some Valium and put my feet up, getting ready to watch one of the many shows I had on my computer.

There was a knock on my door and at the same time I heard the knock, Vegor opened it, his head peering inside. I caught eye contact with him and as I did, a ball the size of my fist flew gently through the air.

I caught it while looking at him.

'What is this?' I asked.

'A trade for tobacco,' he said closing my door.

I opened the packet he had thrown at me. It was huge, as big as my fist. Soft black sticky hash. I got up and walked to Vegor's cabin.

'This is huge,' I said, my eyes pulling my head forward towards the ball in my hand, the realization I could now smoke everyday.

'I have a lot,' Vegor said, 'this is nothing and thanks for the tobacco, you saved me.'

Vegor shifted his eyes.

I'll kill fish tomorrow' he said, 'and if I have to throw garbage to the sea, I'll do that too.'

He smiled, and chuckled through the smoke that clouded his cabin.

'But I am not going to piss in my own bed,' he said laughing. 'I sleep in my bed, so I won't piss in it. But I don't live in the ocean so I'll through our garbage there, and I am no fish so I will kill them.'

He laughed harder, highly amused with his comments about fish, garbage and piss in his bed.

I did not laugh, I just looked at the ball of hash in my hand. I then looked at Vegor.

'Ok,' I said.

4. The ending and the beginning

I woke an hour before shift and did I what I always did. I had a long shower and I had a leisurely breakfast and then sat on the sofa with a coffee in my hands and a cigarette burning.

Perhaps it was Vegor with his thoughts about fish, the idea they shared something in common with us. I thought it could be the hash, but rarely did I remember my dreams when I smoked. Whatever it was from the moment I woke up I could not stop thinking about it. While I stood in the shower it captured my mind as if it were as real as the water that hit my skin. Through breakfast and now sitting here it played over in my mind and I could focus on nothing else. I sank into the comfortable leather of the sofa and thought about the dream I had had. I dreamt I was a school of fish.

I had dreamt that I was a whole school of fish and I was looking through all of their eyes. I was looking through the eyes of thousands of fish. I was them all and we all moved together perfectly. I moved in perfect synchronization. At the exact same moment thousands of fish changed course. Our awareness was shared between each other and I had looked through many eyes and many eyes had looked through me.

It was calm. It felt good being the fish. So much that I was. So many. Shared unity through the fish, each one looking through the eyes of the group. Such a feeling flowed between each member of the school.

I put down my coffee and let my cigarette burn, feeling the feeling that is shared between the fish.

It was calm.

It was exciting.

We all gave ourselves to each other, so much that we shared the same eyes. I had the power of thousands, such a change from my normal human perception. Through this school of fish, I could only share myself with others, and they could only share themselves with me and this was their natural state. This school did not have the ability to be separate from each other.

I looked around the room at all who sat in the mess.

Like we are separate, and as I thought that, as I looked at the men absorbed in food or TV—Dimitri came loudly into the room.

'These new kids,' he said, his voice echoing through the mess. 'They fuck with me!'

An intense distress had swollen his eyes and although he spoke directly to one man, his voice was loud enough and he was angry enough for everyone to pay attention.

'I told him to clean the deck. I told him to throw the garbage overboard, and he did not do it! I told him again and you know what he went and did?'

The room fell silent as all who were present listened.

'He put the garbage on top of the bridge!' Dimitri yelled.

Everyone that was present in the galley was listening and after Dimitri said Vegor put the garbage on top of the bridge, everyone was laughing. I was laughing too. He would not live this down. How could this kid be that stupid?

I left my coffee and went outside.

I climbed the ladder to the top of the bridge, and sure enough there was the garbage. I stared at it. Never before had this occurred, piles of garbage up here. To keep garbage on the ship was an oddity, and I stood staring at it.

The northern lights were showing, huge smoky lines of swirling green and pink across the sky. It was not always that we saw them, even when fishing far north and I watched, looking up to the sky. I liked watching these colours and I thought to make a joint and sit here a while. I looked at my watch and realised I couldn't. I looked back at the garbage and I understood what Vegor thought, to put the garbage here and throw it away when we arrived back to land.

I threw the garbage to the sea.

The bags burst open as they fell from such a height and a scatter of trash both sank and floated away. I watched the debris of paper, tin and plastic float as birds attacked them searching for food.

I went back downstairs and gave relief to the man going off shift.

He was tired, the tank was full and every hook was a big fish. I was fresh and my energy was high. The older man handed me his knife, blowing out a largely exaggerated sigh of relief, hunching his back and shoulders, making himself look as exhausted as possible.

Like many men who have worked at sea their whole life, they do so for that is what there is along the Norwegian coast. I looked at him, he was strong, but I saw such work pushed in a way it never pushed when he was younger. He laughed as he straightened his back and was smiling as he hosed the blood from his weather pants and jacket.

A stream of cool focus swept me.

Time to work. I looked at the wooden gaff in my hand—the steel spike attached to the handle was becoming dull and loose from the timber so I threw it in the ocean and took a new one. Stick the fish, bring them aboard and cut their throats—repeat. Fish after fish, there is no time to stop; there is no time to look away, only you and the rhythm. Stick and cut, stick and cut.

The light attached to the upper deck shines down on the line, allowing you to see which direction the line is coming from under the water, and you can see the fish attached to the line looking as nothing more than shiny white colour as their bodies reflect the light. I looked down and saw something big, it was not a codfish, it was too big. I slowed down the line for it was probably a large Halibut.

Halibut can be huge and weigh more than a man, they are strong and once they exit the water, a flick of their muscular body will free them from the hook and they will swim fast, back to the bottom of the ocean.

I stopped the line and took the long piece of steel with a hook on its end used to hook through the fishes jaw before it comes out of the water and avoid losing such a valuable fish. I moved the line slowly to the surface but it was not a Halibut. It was a dolphin, and It had been caught, the line wrapped around its tail.

I pulled it aboard, freed the line from around its tail and let it sit behind me, then continued to bring the fish on. I saw it was female, the genitalia similar to that of a human. The animal was dead but still fresh and although the ship was busy with a huge amount of fish, I did not like to waste such good meat.

The fish kept coming, never before had there been so many big codfish. Every hook, five-kilo, ten-kilo, twenty, forty, fifty! The fish came like this all day. I was sweating, I was tired and when young Vegor came to change with me I wondered how he was going to manage. I was working as fast as my rhythm was working and I looked at Vegor almost sympathetically. How could he find rhythm enough to bring on and kill so many fish, when he could not even kill them?

I slowed the line down for I didn't expect him to work as fast as myself and I handed him my knife.

I stood hosing the blood from my weather clothes, watching as the fish came aboard and as fast as they were, they were being killed and thrown to the tank of water. I walked back to Vegor. He did not have time to look at me, he did not have the rhythm enough to break his concentration and talk, but he was doing well. He was bringing the fish aboard and what's more he was killing them. Good for him I thought.

I stood watching for a few minutes, and seeing he looked comfortable on his own I dragged the dolphin away to fix it.

Taking the meat from this animal is basically the same as filleting a fish as the meat runs along either side of its spine and underneath the belly of the animal are its organs, just like a fish. I tied some rope to its tail and hoisted it up around a fixed strong point above my head and cut the animal's throat. The blood was warm and steam rose from it as it hit the cool air inside the ship. The blood ran through the holes of the grating floor and washed overboard.

I went and mended some line, giving time for the blood to exit the animal's body, then sharpened my knife well as Dolphin skin is thick. Their skin is coarse like sandpaper, rough to the thin skin of the human hand. Its face and body covered with scars. I looked at the scars. It must have lived a rough life as the skin is thick, and the scars covering it were deep. I stood with my blade, about to cut along the animal's spine when I thought about the dream I had had. I wondered how it must be to live as such an animal. So streamlined and pleasing to look at. I held the knife down.

It sees through eyes. It sees through eyes as I do. It does things as I do. It moves, doing whatever it does, as I do. Only it does so in this streamline form of an animal and it does so in a big salty ocean. I placed the knife back to the animal's spine and I wondered what this animal did with its time. Perhaps it knew what happiness was. Perhaps it knew pain. I looked at the scars covering its body. How dangerous to live in the world down there, all but a huge soup of creatures with mouths of sharp teeth. Predators, eating one another. Prey, being eaten by another.

How easy it is to be human. We have no predators. We have nothing to fear. We have nothing to hide from.

Then as Dimitri turned the corner, I thought, that the one thing we fear is ourselves. The only threat to our self is our self. We overwhelmingly dominate the entire planet. Not only is there no competition or threat from any other species, we are fighting against ourselves to keep in existence species we are killing off. Species we are not even trying to kill, they are just in the way. As Dimitri stood there, I could only think, that it is not through intelligence that we dominate this world. It is simply that we are capable of doing so.

Dimitri looked at the dolphin. He stuck a finger into the animal and laughed—it was, apart from the coarse skin, very similar to human. He slapped the animal on the backside and smiled, then walked through the bulkhead to where Vegor was working.

He saw Vegor and turned back to me.

'You do this now?' he said. 'That little insect is alone losing our fish and you take this meat now!'

His face was growing red and his voice was rising.

'How can you let that new kid stand there in that much fish while you do this now?'

He pointed his finger at me and his voice rose further. 'Is there something wrong in your head? he said. Are you as dumb as this dolphin!?'

His lips were shaking and he was trying to control himself but he was like a thousand Chinese fireworks that had just been lit, and his fuse was burning down.

The calm pool of black tar inside me just got a rock thrown in it, and it splashed. A surge that was calm and asleep woke up. The black pool became hot and heat tingled in the bottom of my toes and flushed me to the top of my head. Hot and boiling. Blackness expanding looking for an exit. From my toes to my head it surged and my face went as red as the blood from this animal.

I pointed the large knife at Dimitri.

'Speak to me like that,' I said. I leaned forward. 'Speak to me again like that,' I said, pointing the large knife at him.

He said nothing and I stuck the knife into the dolphin and walked off.

I rolled a cigarette, and as I took out my lighter I heard Dimitri's voice echoing through the steel walls of the ship. I lit my cigarette, inhaled and listened. I could not make out his words but I was fairly certain he was again yelling about the rubbish Vegor had put above the bridge. I smoked a whole cigarette and still he continued.

I could take no more. I stood up, ready to stop this yelling when Russ came up from the engine room. He was carrying a bucket with dirty oil filters and his coveralls were the usual mess from grease and filth, a big smile was upon his face

'We never seen fishing this good,' Russ said happily. He put down the bucket. 'We're going to be home early at this rate,' he said, but before he could express his wishes for a few days surf trip to the Moroccan coast, he paused and removed his earmuffs.

'What the hell is all that yelling?' he asked.

'Dimitri,' I said. 'He is angry with the new kid Vegor, because instead of throwing the garbage to the sea he put it on top of the bridge.'

'He did what?' Russ asked.

'He put the garbage on top of the bridge,' I said, 'because he didn't want to throw it into the ocean.'

Russ began laughing. 'Something is wrong with that kid,' Russ said, pulling out a packet of cigarettes.

I took one.

We ignored the voice of Dimitri as he continued to yell and agreed on some days surfing along the Moroccan coast, as we would be home early if the fishing continued to be good. I threw the cigarette butt to the floor and looked at Russ.

'I'm tired of this yelling,' I said, and I walked forward to where Vegor was working and Dimitri was yelling.

Russ grabbed my sweater and pulled me to face him, he said nothing and he didn't have to. I saw in his face what his words didn't say. He said with his eyes, he said with the pressure he applied on my sweater. He said I see the heat in your face and the boiling under your skin.

Dimitri stopped yelling when we walked upon them.

Russ poked around the machinery, a second nature to inspect that all was running smoothly. I looked at Dimitri who said nothing, his face was red, his lips were tightly closed. I looked at Vegor. He was sweating hard, his face was red too, but his face was red from work and underneath his sweat and tired eyes he looked calm, and he was doing just as good a job as when I had left him. He had sped the line up to a normal speed and was working well—fish, fish, fish, fish, fish. He was in the zone, he had found his rhythm and he was bringing the fish on and cutting them perfectly, and he was doing so while a big angry man stood beside him yelling abuse.

I laughed.

I laughed aloud, I laughed so hard that Russ, Vegor and Dimitri looked at me.

Vegor smiled and Russ showed an expression of concern. Dimitri turned to me his face red consumed with anger. 'What is funny,' he demanded.

I could not stop laughing.

'Look I said,' pointing at Vegor. I pointed at the job he was doing. 'Look how busy he is,' I said, 'he is doing a good job!'

'So because he does what he is supposed to do that means it is ok to put garbage on top of the house?' Dimitri yelled over the top of me.

He was pointing his finger at me and behind him Russ stared at me.

'And you,' he said, 'you let this little insect stay here while you play with that dolphin back there! You are as stupid as each other!' Dimitri said, and then turned to Vegor. 'Push me again,' Dimitri said. 'Push me again and you will see what will happen.' He stormed off yelling, yelling that echoed through every corner of the ship.

I looked at my watch, it was time for lunch and any minute a relief would come and Vegor and I would go upstairs and eat.

Dimitri came back with his weather jacket on. He was to bring the fish on and we were to go to lunch. He did not look at us, but said only, 'move.'

Vegor stepped aside and Dimitri stepped to take his place and as Dimitri did, he shoved Vegor. It wasn't hard but as the boat rolled gently to one side, Vegor stepped to one foot and lost balance. Vegor lost balance and fell forward. He fell forward onto the blade in Dimitri's hand. The blade in Dimitri's hand was facing up and Vegor fell onto it—the sharp knife cut easily through the side of Vegor's weather garments.

As soon as the knife had cut through both his pants and jacket, Vegor examined his clothes. He looked at Dimitri. He looked at the knife in his hand.

Dimitri looked at Vegor's clothes and continued working. 'Are you stupid kid?' Dimitri said. 'You're going to get a knife in your side if you're not carful, idiot kid! How stupid can you be?' Dimitri waved his knife for Vegor to leave.

Vegor left and hosed the blood from his clothes, careful not to spill water through the now large holes exposing his underclothes.

I stared at Vegor as he hosed off the blood. Then I stared at Dimitri. I stood staring at him. I stood watching him work. He was too busy to turn around and he did not know I watched him. I watched him and I did not move my eyes. I watched him until the cook would be packing up dinner, and not once did I see him do that again. Not once did he rest his knife the way he had when he had shoved Vegor. I stood looking straight to the back of him, waiting for him to rest his blade the same way, but he did not.

Not even close.

It was not an accident.

He had tried to land his blade to Vegor's body, but had missed.

My blood boiled. It rushed, pumping through my body and pressure filled my head. Throbbing pressure. Throbbing blood. Throbbing my eyes. Throbbing my ears. Black hot throbbing. I heard nothing of the loud machinery in progress. No sound, only throbbing. I heard nothing but hot blood throbbing through the walls of the ship.

I walked towards him and as soon as he looked at me, I struck him.

I hit him as hard as I could. I hit him with everything I had and it was hard. It was very hard. My fist connected perfectly with the centre of his face and I felt my fist sink deep into his lips, nose and eyes. I felt my fist was going to come out the other side of his head. I hit him so good he left the ground. He left the ground and fell backwards. He fell backwards out and over the side of the ship.

My hearing returned instantly as I heard the awful splash that was the repercussion of what I had just done.

My heart raced into my face as I looked at the cold ocean and watched his body float down the side of the ship towards the stern. The skipper whilst backing down the ship yelled over the intercom—surprise filling his voice.

'What the hell is this?' he yelled. Followed by notifying the rest of the ship that there was a man overboard.

Time felt like it stopped as I watched his body, face down and still in the icy water.

Panic. The real meaning of panic, when something so bad happens the repercussions are fatal. Stabbing panic, when you are the one that caused it. It is strong and it cannot be stopped, when you are responsible for the death of another man. I was not accustomed to this. Being witnessed hitting another man into the sea. Being responsible for this. This was not normal and my heart froze.

I grabbed the rope ladder and threw it over the side of the ship. I took a sling and climbed down as the ship backed up, Dimitri's limp body drifting toward me in the icy water. I tied the sling around his chest and the other men who were now on deck pulled him aboard.

Shock ran through me. His face did not look good. Stabbing shock. His jaw sat on a huge angle, as did his nose and I looked at his bloody mouth to see teeth were missing.

Shock.

My body was shaking. I stood looking down at him and all I could think was how completely fucked I was. A huge problem. I knelt down, he still had pulse and the moment he opened his eyes, massive relief swept through me.

My heart rate changed from a thousand beats per second to a hundred and my thoughts changed from what a complete dreadful mess I was now in, to simply, what a mess I was now in.

The skipper came down and looked at him. 'Carry him to the sauna,' he said.

The skipper looked at me, he looked at me hard and walked off. We took Dimitri to the sauna and the skipper came with medical supplies and telephone. He turned the element on low as he cut off Dimitri's wet clothes and wrapped him in dry towels.

The skipper put the phone on speaker and let it sit on the floor, discussing with the doctor his condition. It did not sound or look good. The skipper looked directly at me. He stared so hard I thought his soul would leap out of his body and slap me.

'Were going to shore' he said, 'we will drop this mess to land and get back fishing.' He continued to stare at me as he pointed to the door. 'Put a buoy on that line,' he said.

The captain's eyes did not leave me as I left the sauna. How one moment can change everything. I cursed myself as I jogged downstairs.

The line was still attached to the ship, hooks with fish on them waiting to be brought on. But now because of me, we were releasing the line back to the water. Because of me we were to stop fishing. We were not making money, we were only wasting time and I would be charged with the damage I had caused Dimitri.

I cursed myself as I took some line.

I tied it to the line coming out of the water and released the line from around the block. The ship moved forward and I threw out the line. I threw out an anchor. I threw out some more line followed by the buoys and flag and my stomach sank as the ship turned around and headed for the closest Norwegian town.

The ship moved at full speed and as water hit the hull, the salty spray hit and stung my face. No more fishing. No more big fish. No more big fish, hook after hook—because of me. This would cost me a lot, to pay for his face. Certainly my job would be finished here. I rolled a cigarette and looked out over the sea. I wish I could go back, just a few hours back when I was taking the meat from the dolphin.

'Come to the bridge,' the captains voice spoke over the intercom. I thought his voice would split me in half. I felt the speaker would shatter me like glass and then step on me, crushing me into powder. I looked up at the skipper, his one foot on the window he looked through when watching the line, while leaning back as usual in his comfortable chair. I climbed out the hatch and up to the top deck and entered the bridge.

The skipper was a good man. He was soft spoken and in the many years at sea with him, rarely had he raised his voice or lost his temper. Now, I thought, now he surely would.

'What the hell is going on!' he said. He was speaking louder. Now he was raising his voice and again this look. This look I swear meant he would walk right out of his body and shoot me, and not just me, but shoot my soul making sure I was good and dead. His eyes were clear and strong, as piercing as sharp steel. I would rather a blade pushed slowly into my eyeball than look at this man.

My hands were shaking.

My heart was beating.

My hands and heart were shaking with my problem.

I blew out a long breath and began to explain about Dimitri and Vegor, how Dimitri had tried to stick Vegor with his knife, but I was cut off.

The captain waved his arms in front of me, his face looked too pained to listen to me, he looked too pained to hear me talk. 'For God sake,' he said, 'save yourself the breath!'

I stopped talking.

'What the hell Alexander!'

'You hit a man overboard!'

He took a drag from his cigarette while shaking his head.

'You hit a man overboard Alexander!'

He flicked the ash off his cigarette and turned to me explaining with both his hands as he spoke.

'I can have the authorities calling the ship looking for you,' he said. 'You and Russ can destroy all the bars you want when we are in port. You can leave all the men in town unconscious if you want. This is not my problem. This, I could not give a damn in hell about, nor that the sauna stinks of hashish. I care less what you do. But now, now I have to care about this,' the skipper said.

His voice was again calm as he spoke.

'This is now my problem,' he said.

'You are lucky he lived.' He stared at me in disbelief at what had just happened.

'For God's sake Alexander.'

I said nothing.

The skipper flicked the ash off his cigarette, blowing out a deep inhale of smoke.

'I know what Dimitri is like,' the skipper said. 'God knows he deserves every missing tooth he has but for God sake,' he said, 'you hit a man overboard!'

I wanted to sink down—down through every steel level of the ship. I wanted to fall through to the bottom of the ship and pass through the hull and sink to the bottom of the ocean.

I wanted to disappear. I wanted to go back, just a few hours back when I was taking the meat from the dolphin.

There was nothing more to talk about, and I went to leave. The skipper turned to me before I did. 'Are you going to spend the rest of your life doing this?' he asked.

I looked at him.

I closed the door and walked downstairs.

Doing what I thought?

Fishing?

Fighting?

Hitting complete assholes overboard who try to knife people?

I went to my cabin.

I didn't feel like eating. I didn't feel like drinking and I didn't feel like smoking hash.

I felt like sitting in the sauna but Dimitri was there, warming from the cold ocean.

Fucking Dimitri.

5. What comes next?

It did not take long. It was as if I had just sat down, I had to get back up again. I had to tie the ship to the dock and move Dimitri from the ship to the Ambulance. As if it were but a few moments ago I was taking the meat from the dolphin and now we were here. Now this was happening.

The ambulance took Dimitri away and we turned around returning to the lines in the water. One moment, how one moment can change everything.

Fishing was the same. It was the best fishing I had ever seen and despite due to me, being a man short, the crew was not bitter towards me.

They were nicer to me than ever before. Their spirits were lifted and they showed no sighs of displeasure for the extra burden of work. They laughed more and although none but Russ said it, they were pleased Dimitri was off the ship, even if it caused him injury and even if it meant we were a man down.

Russ assured me he was good for nothing and we were all the better for it.

One man I thought, how one man can make a difference to so many. How one man could change the dynamics of the ship. How one man could create tension for all. Vegor was happy; he became friendly with everyone and was always good-natured and always worked hard.

I was glad I hit Dimitri, I was glad he was off the ship. Perhaps he would not have missed sticking a knife into Vegor at a later time?

Every day fishing was the same, huge amounts of fish and as Russ and I suspected we were finished some weeks before Christmas, which meant we had more free time before fishing again in January.

With the freezer full we steamed south towards our homeport, and it was not until we had been sailing for several days, when we were we sufficiently further south, that the sun came over the horizon.

I watched the sun come up; pausing for a moment and then it went back down. For a second I thought I saw the northern lights, green and pink across the sky, I looked again but they were gone.

I sat in the bridge with a coffee and cigarette while the skipper spoke on the radio with a friend on a passing ship. He looked over to me and ended his conversation. He wore a huge smile.

'We have fished better than any ship in the Norwegian fleet,' he said.

He lit a cigarette and threw the packet to the counter top. His eyes shot into me, giving me that same piercing look.

The smile on his face disappeared.

'Dimitri is,' he said, 'apart from recovering from the broken face he collected from you—fine. He does not remember you hit him— only that he woke finding himself in hospital. I have,' the skipper went on, 'explained what happened - that he fell overboard, hitting his head and that the crew did an exceptional job of retrieving him.'

I looked at this man. I stared, lost for words. How could he be so warm? He had just spared my job. I thought about the cost of Dimitri's medical bills and I thought about prison time. Relief ran through me like cold water after the sauna.

But his eyes were not warm.

They were cold. As cold as an ice pick about to push through my neck.

'The ship works better without him,' the skipper said, looking at me and blowing out a long inhale of smoke. The skipper stared into my eyes and I could not look away. You have to change your ways or it cannot end good for you.' the skipper said. 'Look inside yourself Alexander,' he said. 'Look inside yourself for God sake man'. He butted his cigarette, not moving his eyes from mine.

Relief. I could only feel relief.

No hospital bills. No charges.

Just a large cheque from excellent fishing and a surf holiday with Russ.

I felt better than good and that night before arriving to dock, Russ and I filled the sauna with the sweet smell of sticky Afghani hash and talked of plans for our surf holiday.

Russ wanted to go to the Moroccan coast. The food was delicious and at this time of year the waves were strong. I also wanted to go back to this coastline, where we had familiar faces and the surf was brilliant, but as I sank into the wooden bench of the sauna I could only think of going far away. I wanted to go somewhere new, somewhere I had never been before. I wanted to be far away from everything I knew—as far away as possible. I wanted to shatter myself into a thousand pieces and pick myself up somewhere different.

And with the sauna full of smoke, I could only think of a trip to a new and far away land.

'Australia,' I said to Russ, 'or the Americas. Indonesia or the Indian Ocean.' I closed my eyes and let the sweat pour out and the smoke flow in, sinking heavily into the heat of the sauna. Russ did the same, looking as comfortable as I was, and we talked no more about our destination until we were in the bar the following evening, where we sat with the rest of the crew and drank.

With our bags off the ship and in the hotel, the crew spoke of family plans over Christmas while Russ and I, drinking heavily, went over every surf spot on the globe.

6. Futility

The last thing I could remember was that junkie street in Oslo.

My head was pounding. I felt I was being continuously slammed against cement. I could not stand up. I could barely open my eyes.

How in hell did we get to Oslo?

We were on the coast a twelve-hour drive away. I ran over the past but it was blank. Nothing. I remembered leaving the ship and going to the bar, and the last thing after that was that junkie street.

I squinted my eyes and looked around.

Russ was standing by the bank of a river and the sun was crashing down. Russ walked towards me, he was wearing shorts and a large straw hat and he was holding a large bottle of liquid. He placed the bottle in front of me, and I drank eagerly what was a not a bad, but not a good, strange tasting drink. The air was hot, it was humid and sweat beaded off my forehead. I exhaled a huge breath and closed my eyes.

'Where the hell are we?' I asked Russ.

Russ picked up the bottle. 'Damn it' he said, 'this drink is good!'

I rolled over to a pack of cigarettes that lay beside me, and searched my pockets for a light. I pulled out the contents of my pockets and dumped them on the ground. Finding a light and battling the intense throbbing of my head I lit a cigarette. I looked at the contents of my pockets. I had definitely been to that junkie street. I had a bit of everything. Pills, tranquilizers, speed, and there was a ball of heroin.

I picked up the ball and looked at it, wondering how this survived such a journey, to where ever the hell we were? I picked up a packet of pills, it was empty and reading the name on the front I understood why I remembered nothing. I threw it down and gathered from the ground some Valium. I handed half to Russ.

'Where are we?' I asked again. He swallowed them down, chewing as he did with this strange tasting drink. Russ looked at me and began to laugh. He laughed and said nothing. I laughed too but the laughter throbbed hard into my already cracking skull and I stopped, blowing out a long breath, I rolled over, staring into the dirt ground of this unknown place.

Russ pointed at the brown river laughing. He had no idea where we were. I stood up, took a few steps and looked in either direction, but there was nothing, nothing but river and jungle.

I closed my eyes as the heavy thumping inside my head ran through my body. I felt liquid ice had been sprayed into my heart and it was no longer beating but following the throb permeating from my head. Throbbing that felt it would crack at any second and split my skull open, letting ooze out the poison that I had pumped into it. I closed my eyes and heard nothing but the sounds of my skull.

Birds and insects sang, buzzing continuously as sweat beaded from every inch of my body in this tropical weather. I looked at Russ, his shirt was off and his eyes were closed. A picture of his daughter tattooed on his chest and more backyard tattoos covered his arms and stomach, sweat dripping down his skin.

Listening to the sounds of the jungle and feeling this tropical heat, I thought we must be in Asia. Again I tried to recapture any event leading here, but there was none. I remembered only walking that junkie street.

Stumbling as I stepped, I walked away from the river looking for anything other than river and jungle. I breathed deeply as I walked and stopped after a short time when I came to a large clearing. I rubbed and adjusted my eyes. In the middle of the clearing was a small plane. I focused. By the plane was a dark skinned man, wearing an unbuttoned loose fitting white shirt. The sun slammed down increasing the throbbing to my head as I walked towards the plane and this man.

When I approached I saw the man bore a smile as if he were expecting to see me.

'How is everything Mr Alexander?' he asked.

He looked cheerful and was definitely not recovering from the abuse that I was.

'Who are you, and where are we?' I asked him.

The man's smile disappeared. He looked at me as if I had lost my mind, which quite correctly I had, only with the help of every substance available on the streets of Oslo. The man looked at me for a moment then, realising I was serious, he began to laugh.

I liked the way he laughed and I laughed with him, as it was funny. I had ended up in strange places before after getting off the ship and diving head first into the rabbit hole of pills and junk, but never had I ended at a place as this, so different and so far away. Looking around, I was absolutely in the middle of nowhere.

'Christ,' I said.

My head was pounding so hard I had to sit down, my laughter turning into deep breathing. The man stopped laughing as I sat down to breathe, but his smile remained and I could see he was laughing on the inside. He reached into the plane and handed me a bottle of water.

'Strange things happen around here,' the man said, 'and I am no stranger to strange. And as far as strange goes, this is relatively on the lower end of the spectrum'. The man's smile increased. 'However you are the first and I suspect the last two characters who will charter my plane to surf Pororoca, with no boards and when the waves are not even working.'

He could not hold back his laughter any longer, and he let it out, laughing aloud. I stared at him his words sinking in, still I remembered nothing but at least I knew where we were.

Brazil.

Pororoca.

I rested my head in my hands. We chartered this plane to surf Pororoca.

I sat with my head between my knees, massaging my sculp.

The bar.

I remembered sitting in the bar with Russ talking about surf destinations. Damn it.

I remembered wanting to go somewhere new, somewhere far away. Pororoca—definitely far away, definitely somewhere new. I massaged my head.

December, It's December. For Christ sake, that wave is not gonna work here for months to come. I felt my stomach sink like there was a bowling ball inside. How stupid to be here at the wrong time.

I thought about this great wave running for hours through the Amazon River. The longest wave on earth, and we were here at the wrong time.

Why had Russ and I come here now, months before it is due to work and not only that, we had no surfboards. I could recall nothing. My stomach felt sick, sick from my still cracking skull and the bowling ball weighing down inside me.

The pilot leaned against his plane.

'You are a crazy Norwegian man,' he said, 'and you remember nothing.' The pilot smiled. 'I am Gary,' he said, stretching his hand away from his drink. I shook it. 'I am leaving tomorrow,' he said.

I looked at him and I looked at his plane. I looked at the thick jungle. The hot sun crashed down on me.

'Then we would also like to leave tomorrow,' I said.

Gary laughed and through my headache I laughed too. 'Good', he said, 'we go to Sao Luiz tomorrow and tonight you may join some friends of mine for dinner. We shall eat the only food we shall find here, and that is what ever they give us.'

Gary laughed and handed me a large container of the same dark liquid Russ had. 'Drink this' he said. 'I already left some beside you but drink more, it will take away the pain.' I took the container and we arranged to meet back at his plane when the sun had gone down.

I put the container on the ground and sat next to Russ.

'We're in Brazil,' I said.

'Brazil!' Russ said.

'Yeah Brazil, and that guy over there, we got this funny drink from, is a pilot who took us here to surf Pororoca'

'This will take away the pain.' I said—holding the bottle of liquid Gary had given me.

'I know,' Russ said, 'I've been drinking that stuff all morning and damn it if I do not feel excellent.'

Russ stared at me, a blank expression over his face as he computed what I had said and where we were.

'Porocora?' He said.

'Yeah,' I said.

'So we're in the Amazon?' Russ asked.

'Yeah,' I replied.

'So where's the wave?' Russ asked.

'There is no wave, and there won't be until perhaps February,' I said.

Russ looked at me. 'So what the hell are we doing here?'

I looked at Russ.

'We are wasting money on pilots and bad drugs,' I said. Then, it was then, some of my memory returned and I recalled how we had gotten to Oslo.

'We took a taxi to Oslo,' I said.

'We took a taxi? That's an expensive ride,' Russ said, while drinking from the container, 'and I bet that pilot is not cheap either.'

I looked at the pills and junk on the ground. Good for what? I wanted to throw them to the river. Good for spending a month's pay on a taxi and a plane ride. Good for a cracking headache and a container of a strange tasting liquid.

Russ looked at me staring at the ground. 'Don't think about it,' he said, 'Life is good, we are here now, and besides, you cannot fight the waves of life, you can only ride them. We have a good story to tell our children now,' Russ said.

I looked at Russ. 'I don't have children,' I said.

Russ kept smiling and put his hands behind his head and stretched. 'Then you can tell my children,' he said.

Crap, I thought.

Stupid junk. Stupid plane. Stupid taxi. Stupid Dimitri, stupid middle of nowhere place. Working hard killing fish all day for nothing, for nothing but a taxi and plane ride to nowhere. Nothing but a cracking headache and a container of weird liquid to take the headache away.

Russ closed his eyes, somehow finding a happy place amongst the pills and junk that saturated my body. I found no such happy place. All I found was that we had no more tobacco and only half a pack of cigarettes. I felt the weight of the bowling ball sink heavier inside. All I could hear was the words of the captain, his words echoing through my mind. ' Are you going to spend the rest of your life doing this?'

I stood up looking at the brown river. It was the only comfort I had. I needed to change. My stomach felt rancid and my head was throbbing so hard I thought my skull would crack, crack and let run out what ever black soul I had. Letting free my black soul to ooze out and sink to the bottom of this brown flowing river. I sat on the ground, my head falling between my knees, my cigarette falling from my lips and burning into the flesh of my lap. Burning I could not feel. I could only feel the pain that ran through me. I could only feel the cracking of my skull.

I fell deep into the splitting of my skull.

I fell deep into the rancid taste that saturated my stomach.

So much poison. I could not get it out. I wanted to puke but the poison had saturated every organ. I wanted to puke my organs and throw them to the river. I looked at Russ, I wish I could close my eyes and find comfort as he did, but the only comfort I had was the words the skipper used.

The throbbing remained and the rancid taste that filled my stomach remained. I stood up, stumbling as I did and took all that was left of the pills and junk and threw it into the river.

Russ left his comfortable stretched out position and stood up.

'What the hell is this! What the hell are you doing? We are stuck in the middle of nowhere and you throw what little we have away! What is wrong with you?'

I was shaking.

Russ saw the state I was in and he stopped, he just stared at me. 'It's just a downer,' he said.

'Take it easy, we leave tomorrow. It has been worse, just relax,' he said. 'Feel the downer. Don't let it take you down, you are stronger than it.'

I could not relax. It was not ok. All the rancid shit of my life was stabbing my stomach. It was cracking my skull. It surrounded me and it was swallowing me. Dimitri's broken toothless bloody face was about to head butt mine and break it worse than I had broken his. My heart felt it was made from poison and I could do nothing but break down. I wanted to break; I wanted to break myself into a million pieces.

The rancid taste consumed me. I wanted to puke but I could not, I wanted to jump into the river and be eaten by a big snake but that would not help. The only piece of light I could hold onto were the words of the captain. That I could stop being myself and change into someone else. I shook.

Russ just looked at me. He lit me a cigarette and handed me the container of brown liquid. 'Drink this,' he said. 'I'll be dammed to know what it is, but it took away my downer.'

I took a large gulp and put the bottle down.

'Drink it all Alexander.' Russ pushed the bottle back to me and I drank heavily, finishing what tasted like a slightly bitter not good but not bad herbal water. I fell back to the ground.

Russ closed his eyes and told of how nice it was not to hear the noise of the loud diesel engines. I felt the brown liquid swirl gently in my stomach as I listened to the passing water. I felt my stomach settle. The bowling ball was melting and my headache was fading. I listened to the insects, to the birds and soon my headache was gone. All pain was gone, gone like it was never even there. I looked at the empty container on the ground and then at Russ who looked as comfortable as ever with his feet stretched out and his eyes closed. He was right, that's for sure; this drink does take away pain. I felt good. My stomach felt calm and my heart felt clean and I assumed the same position as Russ, closing my eyes and stretching out my feet listening to the relaxing sounds of the river.

Air, for the first time since finding myself here, I felt the air I was breathing in.

Delicious tasting air.

7. Something new and strange

We woke up to Gary standing over us, pretending to knock as if there was an imaginary door. I stood up. I felt rested. I felt fresh.

Gary had buttoned his shirt, and stood with an older man who must have lived here for he had no shirt and across his face and chest was some kind of tribal tattoo work.

Russ looked excited and turned to me smiling. 'So this is the dinner call?' he said.

Gary introduced the old man as a member of the tribe that lived on this land. He said that this man was responsible for preparing the medicine we drank, and that he was glad we were looking better.

I looked at this old man.

He stood strong. I had not seen a man like him before. I turned to Gary, 'he made that drink?' I asked.

'Yes,' Gary said, 'and you are welcome to join them for dinner, but he wants to know what you think you are doing here.' I looked at Gary.

'You know what we are doing here,' I said. 'You brought us here. Christ, Gary. We are two stupid Norwegian men who have taken every possible combination of drugs we get our hands on and we follow impulses based on stupidity leading to my heart feeling like poison and my skull feeling like an earthquake. To here, the middle of nowhere. Tell him that, Gary. That is why we are here.'

Russ turned to me, giving me a comical agreeable look. 'You know,' Russ said, with a smile, 'that is a pretty good explanation of why we are here.'

Gary turned to the small tattoo covered man and conveyed what I told him. The old man looked at us both.

He had a look I had not seen on a Norwegian man before. He had a look I had not seen on any man before. It was a look that said many things. It was a look that said I live here. It was a look that said I know who I am, I know what I am and I know the ground I walk on. It was a look that said I am gentle yet I am ferociously strong and nothing can shake me from who I am.

He studied both Russ and me thoroughly, staring at us as through he were reading the fine print of a newspaper. He went over every part of our bodies, searching, reading with his eyes. Reading and looking into the space around us as intensively as he did stare into our eyes. I was captivated by this man.

He came to me and put his hands on my wrists then slid them down and held my hands for a moment. He patted me on the chest and did the same to Russ, then talked with Gary in his language.

No man had ever looked at me like this before. He was neither aggressive, nor was he submissive, he appeared simply to be studying us. I looked at Gary for a translation and Gary cleared his throat.

'My friend, whose family live on this land, says you are welcome to join them for a meal tonight.' Gary cleared his throat again. 'He says he has heard about the people from the other lands. He says he has heard they are sick and that they do not even know what they are, that they do not even know what is the ground they walk on. He says he never believed it could be true, but now, after meeting you two, he sees it. He sees how badly damaged you are, and he says he has some medicine that will help you.'

The old man opened his mouth shining us a great smile as he nodded his head, but Russ did not smile.

'Are you kidding me?' Russ said.

The old man reached his hand to Russ's shoulder, nodding whilst patting him on the upper arm. I stared at this old man. Already I knew that his medicine worked. Never before could I feel so good after such a huge dive. That drink, that drink he had made for us, the drink Gary had given me. I wanted to share a meal with them.

8. The magic begins

It was dark and we followed a not so frequently travelled path through rather thick jungle. The noises surrounding me were unlike anything I had heard before. Such activity and such noises I did not know existed, creatures I could not see. Creatures I had never heard before. We walked in silence and I listened.

The old tattoo covered man led the way, and then stopped. Before us, connected from one side of the path to the other, was a large spider and web. Its back, head and legs shimmering different colours as it lay still on its web. I moved my face close but a hands width away and looked over its every detail. I did not know such spiders existed. I put my hand out and extended my fingers measuring exactly how big this spider was.

The old man watched me, studying me as I studied the spider, his eyes were unflinching, and with the tattoos etched across his chest and face he looked fearsome, yet his eyes were gentle. I had never seen such eyes on a man.

I knew the sounds of the ocean and I knew the coast. I knew the Norwegian fjords and I knew my way around the towns the ship docked in. I knew where we took oil, where we offloaded our catch and where the bars were, but never had I seen such a spider. I had never heard the jungle. I looked at the spider holding to the complex web it had spun. This was the old man's world and the jungle was his home. He knew the spider and he knew the path, and he knew the sounds that came from the jungle. I was different here. I was the one out of place, and he studied me as I studied the spider and like a parent letting a child explore, as soon as I had seen enough and pulled my eyes away, he continued.

The spider's web that crossed our path was attached to trees on either side. The old man looked for a moment, before picking up the lines of the web. He took one string with one hand gently between his thumb and forefinger and took another line with his other hand. He detached the web from one of the trees and holding the line taut, so as not to collapse it, he took a step back, removing the spider's web and swinging it to one side as if it was a door.

The three of us passed and he reattached the spider's web to its original position. He walked to the front of us and continued. I looked back at the spider. It had not moved and sat still in the centre of its web. It was unaware of the near danger it had encountered. It was unaware of how lucky it had been, lucky to live, lucky not to have to spin a new web. I looked at the spider, its colourful body and web shining in the light of the moon. This spider was lucky. This spider was lucky it did not encounter me. This spider was lucky that I or anyone else from my world had not been leading the way on this path. They may not have seen the spider and walked right into it. They would surely not have detached and reattached its web. They would not have. They would have thought only of their path. They would have thought only of the path they were walking and how the spider was in their way.

How detailed its web was. Such a form. This spider sitting on its creation. Its colourful body shone and I wondered how it was to see through its eyes. I thought of my dream, looking through the eyes of fish and I thought of Vegor, how he did not wish to kill them. I looked at the spider, wondering what it would be like to be such a creature and sit on such a web. I turned from the web expecting to hurry to catch up to the others, but they stood waiting and the old man's eyes were locked on me as mine had been locked on the spider.

He turned and walked and we followed. We walked and I thought of what this man had said, how the other lands were sick. I thought of the spider and I thought of Vegor and the fish. I watched this old man walk through the jungle. Never had I seen a man walk like him. He walked as if he were in a shop of china. He walked as if he were in a shop of precious items that were breakable and important. He walked as if he had a backpack on his back, walking between slim isles of balancing teapots he did not wish to break. He was exact of his every movement. He was firm and gentle with every step he made, touching, as he walked, the trees and plants beside him. He looked around in ways I hadn't seen before, running his fingers along the trunks of trees. He squeezed gently the leaves of plants and touched their stems. He touched them as if he knew them. He touched them as an owner would pat their dog or say hello to a stranger. Touching them as a lover might play with their partner's hair. He touched them in the same manner a scuba diver might when exploring a brightly coloured underwater world.

We continued a while longer until we came to a small clearing, where sat a long house, constructed of timber and a roof of leaves, held together with vines. It was dark but the moon was big and I could see there was space cleared where vegetables grew.

We entered and were greeted by the old man's wife, a small woman also bearing similar tattoos to her face and body. She had a fire inside and the fragrance of cooking came in from another section of this long house. We sat by the fire and were joined by two younger men of a similar age to Russ and I, and with them was an older man, who was much older than our host.

Gary translated as the old tattoo covered man who called himself; 'Pi' introduced us to his two youngest sons and father. Their house was clean and homely and they had a few western items, which

Gary explained he brings whenever he comes to the area, some cooking utensils, glassware and clothing. Gary looked proud at explaining this and Pi looked equally proud, showing off the axe he had standing in the corner of the room.

His wife set down a clay pot that Pi took. He dipped a pottery cup into it and filled it with liquid. Gary was an excellent translator as Pi, taking drink from the clay cup, explained that his wife made absolutely the best drink that there was. Gary pointed to the pot of liquid. 'This drink is made from a type of root vegetable, similar to potato and it is slightly fermented.' Gary took a drink from the clay cup and looked at both Russ and I, then put the cup down.

He looked around the room warmly towards Pi and his family and, although they could not understand our language, their attention was focused as if they understood every word.

'Life is different here,' Gary said. 'What life means is different here.' Gary raised his hands slightly. 'What spiders plants and fish mean is different here, what we mean is different here. What it means to be here and what it means to be human is not what it means in other parts of the world. There is no mine or yours here,' Gary said, 'there is no such thing as ownership.' Gary took another drink.

When I told them, that people over the rest of the world own land and own things, they looked at me puzzled. They did not understand. How could people believe such? How could they be in such disarray, that it seemed possible for them to own a piece of the surface of the earth? They did not understand such a concept.

They shook their heads when I told them—sick they said, these people are sick. They do not know themselves and they do not know the earth that they walk on'

I told them that where we come from we have poured concrete over the land and built tall buildings.'

They asked me 'why?'

'So we can travel faster across the land', I told them.

They asked me where we went?

'We go to work', I told them.

They laughed!

Sick, they said. A world of beings who don't know themselves and who don't know the earth.

Tell them you own the land here, and they will tell you—you do not know the land that you walk on.'

The pot was passed around and we all took and drank from the same glass, as Pi's father and his two sons examined Russ and I the same way Pi had. The smell of food wafted in form the other room and I felt my stomach rumble and my mouth water a little.

We talked for some time, sharing through Gary's translation both the ways they live and how they spend their days. They told us of their family dynamics and we told them of ours. We told them of the ship we work on and the huge amount of fish that we caught. We told them of the sun that never went down in the summer and the long dark winters that covered the land with snow. They listened attentively when we spoke and our conversation ended when Pi's father after saying a few words, stood and left the room. Pi spoke and motioned for Gary to explain what his father had said.

Gary turned to us. 'He wants to give you some medicine.'

I turned to Gary. 'I feel good', I said, 'my headache is gone after drinking the medicine you gave us'.

'This is different,' Gary said.

Pi's father came back in the room and placed a stone in the fire. His two sons left and Pi and his father talked at some length with Gary. When they finished, Pi motioned for Gary to translate.

Gary looked at Russ and I, not shifting his gaze. He pressed his hands together and pointed his fingers towards us. 'This is very strong,' he said. 'It is used for cleaning and for bringing love into your life.' Gary's eyes looked deep into ours. 'This medicine is a connection with the spirit world. It is a connection to the earth. It is a connection to yourself and to the stars'.

Gary paused.

I looked at Russ, who seemed more captivated by the smell of food coming from the other room than some tribal spirit medicine.

I was captivated by Pi. I was captivated by the way he looked at me. I was captivated by the way he had handled the spiders web and by the way he walked through the jungle. I turned to Gary. 'How can medicine bring you love?' I asked.

Gary turned to Pi and spoke for a short time before returning to me.

'Love,' he said, gesturing towards Pi, 'is our natural state of being and we are,' Gary said, 'always living in love. However, we step away from this flow whenever we stop living in harmony with whomever or whatever we interact with. We step away from the love that's the binding force with all of life whenever we put our self or others into some kind of perception or judgement. When we stop them from becoming anything other than what we recognise them to be. When we do this we step away from the river that flows between us and we fall deeper into the physical world. We step into our own perception. We step into what we recognise and into our own judgement.

Then you will not hear the trees in the forest for they will be nothing but wood. You will not hear them, not because they do not speak. You will not hear because you are not listening. We step away from the world of spirit, falling blindly into our own illusions of the concrete physical world.'

Pi spoke again and Gary turned back to me and translated.

'Like the spider on the path,' Gary said, 'or, like the path that came to the spider. There was an opportunity for Pi to step out of this flow of love. He could have stepped out of the connectivity that runs through all beings and destroyed the spider's web. He could have stepped into his own separate illusion. He could have stepped into any possible relationship with the path and the spider. He could have killed it. However, to live through your own judgements of this world is to step away from that which connects us all. This is why Pi says—you and others from your world are sick. For you have stepped away from harmony with yourself, from others and the earth you walk on.'

'This medicine will clean you,' Gary said. 'It will clean you from the reasons you have stepped away from harmony with the earth and all beings and it will free you from the pain this is causing you.' His eyes did not move from ours, trying to persuade us of the intensity this medicine would bring. 'Both Pi, and his father, are medicine men,' Gary said, 'and they know the medicinal plants of this jungle and they treat those who live on this land, and people come a long way to see them.'

Gary unbuttoned his shirt and slid his arm free from one side. He moved closer to Russ and I, revealing a scar. It was huge, running from his lower stomach across his side and up his back. The scar was brutal and Gary explained that some fifteen years ago he emergency landed his plane in the clearing we had walked from.

Gary leaned forward as he explained.

'I was flying a load of equipment to an oil company's drilling site. The company stressed how urgent the components were and that they could not continue without them. I was young and I was not comfortable with the condition of the aircraft I had at the time, but they offered me such a huge sum I could have bought a new plane, so I took the load and made it this far.' Gary smiled and began to chuckle. 'You want to talk irony,' he said. When I emergency landed, the machined steel I was carrying to the oil company's drill sight came hurling from the back of the plane, and shot through the back of my chair.' Gary lifted his shirt again showing us the full extent of the scar he had acquired from the steel piece. I stared at it. It was the largest scar I had seen before.

'I woke up,' Gary said, 'in a house similar to this one, and everyday Pi and his father would clean and pack medicinal plants into my wounds. For one month I lay sustaining a broken leg and a broken arm and a wound so deep it was exposing my insides. They fed me and gave me different medicines to drink until I felt even better than when I had arrived.' Gary smiled towards Pi and his father.

'I stayed a long time after I was better, learning the language they speak and learning a new way of life. I grew a love for these people. I grew a love for the love that they have for each other and a love for the land that they live on. Now I visit as often as I can. I stopped deliveries for the oil companies and when you two insisted on coming here, despite my attempts to convince you there was no wave to surf. I let you have your way.'

I stared at Gary. 'How persistent were we?' I asked.

'To see for yourself if there was a wave or not?' Gary asked.

'Yes,' I replied.

Gary chuckled.

'You said you would buy my plane and fly it yourself. You said if I would not fly you and if I would not sell you my plane, you would get another anyway.'

Gary looked strongly at Russ and I. 'They are powerful medicine men and when I crashed my plane here, I got more than just physical healing. These men know what they are doing and believe me what they are doing is out of this world.'

Pi's father was shuffling the fire in the room, separating the wood from the hot coals. The fire was dwindling and the room was becoming darker. His old heavily wrinkled face was visible through the dim light of the room and he looked as strong as a large standing rock. He shuffled the fire. Slowly we were moving into the darkness.

'It was no accident I landed here,' Gary said. 'It was no accident that the very item I was flying to the drill site had nearly taken my life. The very item that was to play a part in the continued destruction of this land had nearly killed me.' Gary looked towards Pi and his father. 'These people saved my life. They saved my life through the connection they have with the very land I was setting out to destroy.' Gary looked from Pi and his father to Russ and I.

'There is no coincidence in life,' Gary said. It was no coincidence that I arrived here.' Gary paused. 'And it is no coincidence that you are here.'

Pi's father rolled over the glowing coals in the ash of the fire and spoke as the room became darker.

'He said he knew you were going to arrive here,' Gary said. 'He says that you asked to come see him.'

I looked at Gary. 'He thinks I asked him to come here?' I said.

Pi's father began chuckling.

'We are always talking through the universe,' Gary said. 'When we step away from harmony with the universe and into our own perception of our own individual reality, we can only see through the eyes of a very small piece. We can only see the world with the perception we have given it. We can then not see the interactions we are having behind the curtains.'

'However, to be more precise,' Gary said, 'it was not only that you asked to come. You were invited, and both his invitation and your request to come here were made and accepted at the same time.'

There was only a glow remaining in the fire, and aside from the moonlight shining through the cracks of the walls, the room was black.

I forgot about eating and I forgot about the smell of food as Pi's father shuffled towards me. He was holding the glowing rock from the fire the size of an apple in his hand. It was glowing bright red and smoke drifted from it in front of his strong solemn face. He leaned towards it his lips almost touching the glowing rock and he blew. The smoke blew gently from the glowing rock towards me, his eyes looking deep into mine, penetrating eyes that seemed to want to enter my soul. His breath pushing smoke, hazing towards me in the dark room and as I breathed in I felt them both enter.

The smoke and his breath entered and I felt something unlike anything I had felt before, unlike anything I even thought was possible to feel. Smoke and breath that seemed to have a mind of its own. And it moved inside me as if it were looking. Pi's father held the glowing rock towards Russ and blew and I watched the smoke head straight for Russ as if it knew where it was going. I felt the smoke and I felt the breath, it 'was' looking, and it seemed to be becoming familiar with where it was.

Pi came and sat before me, he knelt close as the smoke moved around the room and inside me.

It moved easily and smoothly through me. Like a drop of green dye. One drop to a glass of water, slowly encountering every element until the entire glass is coloured green. This smoke flowed, reaching through every part of me. I felt it creeping through every cell, searching through every corner.

Pi straightened himself in front of me and raised both hands in the air. He shook his hands slightly, the vibration of which ran through his body. His whole body was shaking slightly. He cleared his throat. He cleared his throat and began humming, quiet and soft, a deep humming. A vibrational humming that matched his shaking. Calm melodic humming.

Then.

The smoke woke up!

It woke up to Pi's humming and it paid attention. It gripped me. I paid attention. It gripped every piece of me and it vibrated.

Humming, the smoke inside me was humming. The smoke was awake and it was humming with Pi.

They had given me a medicine that was alive.

Pi had fed me a snake and he was the charmer. I felt it was dancing with him. I felt Pi was dancing with it and I was feeling them both. Pi had given it a body to be in, my body, and it vibrated with every part of me, holding me with it, holding me to the rhythm of Pi.

Such overwhelming presence of another filled me. I thought I would burst. I thought I would burst with this energy, the vibration of Pi, and this smoke holding onto every piece of me humming, and then—boom!

Chanting!

Pi 'exploded' into musical chanting and the smoke that filled me truly woke up!

It woke up to Pi's chanting.

Like a cheetah had been crouched humming while positioning itself to its prey, then running fast for what it knew it could take. Sprinting and chanting!

The smoke woke up!

This was change.

It opened its eyes.

The smoke inside me opened its eyes; it opened its eyes to Pi's chanting.

All nine hundred million of them!

My eyes, myself, my smoke, my chanting, me. I was the eyes looking through the smoke that filled me and this smoke was not just in me. It was in everything!

The spirit world.

Me, I was in the spirit world. I looked around. I understood. I had always been in the spirit world; my eyes had just been closed. However now, now my eyes were open.

A medicine that was but a glowing rock in the physical world, my world, the physical world that I knew, however, here it was more. Here I was in its world and here it was a life-force and it was very awake. It was here, through the eyes of this smoke, I saw myself in a way I had not seen before. A way that had been hiding right under my nose.

I felt who Pi was, all of who he was, all of who he was vibrated through me. I felt what he was connected to. Connected to the world, more, everything, Pi was in-tune with and connected to all things and he was bringing me to the same world in which he lived.

A world of such feeling it cannot be explained.

A love so great it is unexplainable. A life-force that connects all things to all things. A life-force that runs through all things. A single life-force.

Us.

I sank into a world of indescribable bliss. Such pleasure. It is indescribable. I did not know such feelings existed, to be a part of and connected to everything. A magnificent being that connects us all. A magnificent being that we are a part of. Bliss. Utter bliss. The love that connects us all. The love that we are.

In my dream, I had seen through the eyes of fish, but this was more. This was much more. I was seeing through the eyes of a part of us all. A part of us woven into all life. A part of us that reached into the earth. A part of us that reached into the stars. Never could I have imagined a world such as this.

A different world.

The spirit world.

Not a world where perception is looking through the two eyes on the head of a being walking this earth. It is not. This part of us lives in a different world. A different place, a place I had never been to before. A place I would never have believed to exist. However, it is there. It is real and Pi knew it.

There was no long house. There was no physical world. However, there was a world and Pi was familiar with it. I had got what I asked for, to be smashed into a million pieces and here I was. Smashed into more than a million.

It was indescribably wonderful.

My pain could not join this world and it was left behind. It was merely something I had been holding onto. Pain that is not even real. Fear and pain, it is not real and cannot exist in this world. The pain I had carried with me my whole life was gone. It could not join me as I looked through the eyes of the magnificent being we are all a part of.

Peace within myself.

The peace of this world.

The happiness of this world.

Indescribable.

Clean. Free. Strong. Happy.

I sat, as Pi kneeled, his hands shaking over me, singing in his language, this vibrational chanting.

He spoke in this world and I felt what he said. I felt his thoughts as I listened with ears I never knew I had. I saw with eyes I had never opened before.

'Change,' he said, 'now you change.'

He stopped singing. He stopped singing and I stopped. I stopped vibrating and I no longer felt him. I no longer felt joined to the vibration of his singing and I felt myself, back, reassembled as me. I felt myself back together. Back as I always had and I felt the same as I did earlier that day, the same as I did earlier with a splitting headache. Only now it was worse. Now it was much worse. Now I felt my skull would actually crack and I would feel it as it did.

I dropped from a world that felt like heaven into a world that must have been hell and I felt pain like I had not felt pain before. I gripped hard into the earth beneath me, so hard I thought I would break my hands with my grip. I felt pain I did not know existed. I could taste pain, I could hear pain and it was unbearable. Nothing could be this strong. Pain burning into every feeling my body could accept and amplified to an intolerable level. If this was not hell then this place was worse, for nothing could be this unbearable. Nothing could be this disgusting to be a part of.

It was every pain I had caused another. It was every destructive thought I had had to another. It was everything I had ever done and every thought I had ever had. It was all here. It was every poison I had thrown to the sea. It was what I had done to others, what I had done to the land and what I had done to myself. It was all here.

This was my day of judgement. True judgement. Myself looking through the eye of that which connects us all, looking at myself. My skull cracked and I felt screaming pain like never before. I thought this pain would surly bring death but it did not. It brought something much worse. I felt my skull crack and a burning river violently smashed into me, flooding me with every action and every thought I had ever made, filling my mouth and lungs as though my head was held into a straight bucket of bleach. Poison pushing in, poison pushing out, poison everywhere, stabbing every piece of me. Blades of hot steel. It was inside me. It was outside me. It was everywhere. I saw with countless eyes and I tasted with countless tastebuds. Sharp glass breaking inside my mouth cutting violently through my insides, opening wounds for the poison to push deeper. The taste of poison, deadly poison. I could not believe this was happening. It was mine and I was soaking in it. It was everywhere, filling every corner of this world. The taste of screaming pain.

I sat there in the long house, in the night, in the heart of the Amazon, lost in myself, and I screamed.

I screamed hard.

A world of poison.

There was nothing else.

A world of poison that went for eternity. There was no escape. I could not leave.

I screamed as loud as I could, but the louder I screamed the louder the poison surrounding me screamed. It screamed so loud it was deafening. So loud. So painfully loud. I could not believe this was happening. A bad dream—I wanted to wake up—I wanted to be anywhere else.

But it was not a dream, it was real and I was not going anywhere.

Emotions and feeling pushed beyond their maximum extent. Monumental. I wanted to pull my hair out, that the blood might sooth the pain.

I called for help but there was no one there. I begged for death, but there was no death in this world. There was nowhere to go and there was no one to help me.

I screamed for it was all I could do. It was the only relief I could find but as I screamed I choked on my own breath. My own breath stuffed with the broken glass I had pushed into the faces of men, choking on the plastic I had thrown to the sea, choking on the filth inside me. I choked as I tried to breathe. I choked trying to scream.

There was no air only filth and poison.

I begged for death to take me away.

On all fours in this longhouse, my hands gripped deeply into the earth, choking on my own screaming I begged for death. Sweating as though a thousand degree sun burned my skin. Shaking and sweating as I gripped the earth beneath me. Shaking and sweating and choking. There was no way out and I could not leave. It was me. I could not leave myself.

Everything I had done, I had done not only to others but I had done to myself. I had created it and it was within me. I was everything I had created and I was living with it. Every soap, bleach and plastic I had thrown to the sea I had been pouring directly into myself and now I was choking on it. I wanted to vomit but I could only choke.

The poison went nowhere. I choked and shook; sweat pouring out of me, lost in this rancid world. Forever, I will be here forever. I was trying to breathe filth, as I shook begging for death.

This must be hell.

I began to cry.

Tears poured down my face in bucket loads. I could not scream and I could not breathe, but I could cry.

I cried so hard I felt I was only my eyes. I felt the poison around me and I felt what it was. Every part of me that I was. I felt it and I cried. The people I had hurt. The people whose lives I had damaged forever. Crushing every part of them. I had hurt people and their lives would never be the same. I felt them now. I felt them now and it is poison.

I cried for what I had done. I cried at the suffering I caused. I cried for the horrible pain I was living with and the poison I had dumped into the sea. I cried in shame. Utter shame. Such love I had stepped away from. Such purity I spat on. I had turned my back on sharing love with the world, and I had been living on drinking the blood of its children. I cried as the poison ate me inside. Tears of shame and tears of pain poured out.

I wanted it gone. I wanted it all away.

I screamed and I cried as loud as I could, as hard as humanly possible. I could never leave this place. There was too much filth.

I could never cry it away.

I could never scream hard enough.

There was nowhere to go.

I was here forever for this was me.

I cried for what felt like a lifetime.

A lifetime.

This felt like a lifetime!

A lifetime of darkness.

Darkness filth and pain.

Every moment I begged for death.

There was no way out. In the darkness of my own poison I begged for death.

I begged for death—but I was already there.

There is only one way out of darkness and through my darkness it came—A light.

A light that shone.

A light that sung.

Through the darkness and pain I cried and I listened.

The most beautiful sound I ever heard.

I was not alone.

Faintly very softly was Pi. Singing. Shining a light in my darkness.

He was singing the sweetest song I ever heard. I cried as I heard the most powerful chant I ever thought possible.

He was here. He was here with me.

Through the darkness and filth he came. He brought light to my world. He brought an endless supply of unlimited strength.

He took me away from the filth of myself.

I wept in my own shame, in my own ignorance at what I had seen of myself.

I wept for the earth and the poison I had poured into it and I wept at the pain I had been inflicting upon others.

I wept for the love I had stepped away from as it surrounded me now, holding me, protecting me from myself.

I put my head to the earth in shame.

Pi and myself, a part of this earth, a part of this world that we are all a part of. This world that I had sucked the blood from, and cast to the sea as a handful of ash. Pi's love ran through me, through my every corner.

Like a man overboard lost in rough sea, his song gave me air, his song gave me hope and strength. It was a song of sorrow and it was a song of pain. It was a song of realization and change. It was through his song that he spoke.

He was laughing.

Through his song he was laughing.

He laughed as he sang and as quickly as I had been taken away from my physical world, I was back. My eyes dried up and before me I could see Pi and he was chanting hard.

He was singing with everything he had.

Again I could see the dark of the longhouse and the moonlight that poked through its cracks. Again I heard his words, spoken to ears I never listened with before.

'You see what you live with,' Pi exclaimed.

'You see what happens when you live like this.'

'You see the love that is here.'

Pi leaned forward and placed a large clay pot in front of me.

I knelt on the dirt floor, helpless to this process as I leaned down sinking my hands into the earth, gripping hard as the flood of poison came back. Poison inside me that was vibrating to a different form that Pi held me to. Poison that could no longer bond with me and had no place to live in my being.

Pi had separated me from my own poison.

He was stronger than my pain, so much stronger.

'Time to come out,' Pi said.

This medicine gripped onto every piece of poison inside me. It gripped onto every pain of the world I had been soaking in and it took hold of it and it exploded out of me as I vomited harder than I ever thought was possible. Bleach, poison, acid, fear, hate, pain, upside down razorblades pushed out by an unstoppable force. I tasted the taste and I felt the feeling. I felt the taste and I tasted the feeling.

All the pain of the world passed through me. All the poisonous pain I had been living with violently pushed out with this medicine.

All night long.

It was all night long, but it felt like a lifetime. I thought I would be there forever but it was only one night.

Morning came.

It was morning when it stopped.

It was not until morning that the effect of this medicine and the horrendous night I had endured ended.

Exhausted.

I sat exhausted.

Sun filled the longhouse and I sat with my sweat-drenched shirt beside me. Pi sat in front of me, his hands on my chest, his forehead pressed against mine.

I heard him.

Who he was passed through me.

'Good,' he said.

'Good.'

'Cleaning,' he said.

'Cleaning.'

Tears poured down my cheeks as I wrapped my arms around this man, my tears dripping to both my bare chest and to his. He wrapped his arms around me holding me as close as I was holding him.

'Brothers,' he said.

'We are brothers.'

'We are all brothers.'

Pi pointed to the clay bowl I had been vomiting into. 'Poison,' he said.

'This is poison.'

'We throw this away,' he said.

He lifted one finger in the air while one hand still rested on my chest.

'We throw this away,' he said, 'and we never make more'

Pi took the bowl and stood up, talking casually with his father as he walked out of the house.

Both Gary and Russ were gone and I lay on the hard floor and breathed. The fresh air of this world. I lay on the floor and listened to the sounds of the jungle.

The sounds of this world. The sounds of my world.

Fresh air.

Fresh air at last.

9. Rebirth

I stood up and exited the longhouse, ducking so as not to hit my head on the small doorway. It was brightening outside and I looked up to see the sun in a still early morning position. Away in the short distance I could hear the flowing of the river

I felt light and walking felt effortless. I felt clean, and I smiled, a big smile, and as I walked towards the sounds of the river I noticed how vibrant everything was. I noticed how alive the trees and plants seemed to be.

They seemed to whisper as I passed them. They seemed to smile at me. They seemed to be laughing and as I walked I felt the ground I was treading on. I followed the sounds of the river.

It felt alive.

Alive as I am.

It seemed to hear what I was thinking, and it seemed to be responding. It was laughing. It was laughing as it was responding. The ground was laughing at me. 'You see,' it said. 'You see what you feel when you don't live with poison.'

I had lived in this world my whole life yet I felt it was the first time I had really seen where I was.

It was obvious and I saw it. I understood and I laughed. It was simple. The trees rooted into the ground, every plant, a part of the same earth. Every insect. Every animal. Every person and every being are a part of the plants. Eating them, breathing with them, all of us, and all of them, are a part of each other. All of everything of this world is together. All animals, all plants and all minerals are all a part of the same world. We are a part of one living being.

The trees around me laughed. The ground underneath me laughed. I could not take my smile away. How could I never have seen this before? It was so tremendously obvious. Of course we are all one, of course we are all a part of the same being. We are so obviously connected.

Pi was right. I was sick. I had lived my whole life with poison. My whole life I had buried my fears and hid them inside, pretending they were not there, living in my own prison. Covering my fear with power, a power made of hate and pain. I had been walking the earth interacting with the world through my hate and pain, constantly pouring more poison into myself. I laughed. It was ridiculous. Completely ridiculous.

I felt the love flowing through the earth and through the trees. I felt it flowing through the plants and through the air. I felt it flowing through me and I understood what Gary had said. Now I understood what he meant.

We are this love.

And it always flows.

We just step away from it when we live through poison. When we live in a way that stops it flowing through us. When we stop it flowing through us and stop it flowing to others. It is that simple.

I was stopping the flow of love whenever I stopped an interaction, any interaction with anything. I lived interacting with the trees and plants through my own perception—nothing but food and nothing but wood. I had never heard them laugh before.

I followed the path to find Russ and Gary sitting on a large rock by the river. They both heard my footsteps and turned around. Russ hopped up immediately and rushed toward me throwing both arms around my shoulders. 'That was the most incredible night of my life!' he said.

Russ looked into my eyes, searching for a response, but I could only smile and as I laughed aloud I felt the laughter run from the ground and shake my stomach. A huge smile appeared across Russ's face and we both sat down on the large rock next to Gary.

I was about to tell Russ what had happened to me. I was about to tell him that I had seen through the eyes of a part of us all and how it is connected to the earth, how it is connected to everything. I was about to tell him how I had entered a world of unimaginable poison and how Pi had separated me from this poison and that I had vomited this poison out of myself and that now I felt new. That now I felt, flowing from the earth and the trees, such life I had never felt before, but before I spoke, Russ began to explain what had happened to him.

Staring at me, Russ looked completely blown away. 'I died,' he said.

He looked into my eyes pausing before he continued, giving me a moment to realize what he had said.

I looked at Russ. Something about him had changed. He sat differently, the way his arms seemed to hang from his body looked different. The way he carried himself had changed. The way he spoke seemed 'new.'

'You died?' I asked.

'Well, I was not here,' Russ said, 'but I was still surely me.'

'I was in a different world.'

Russ blew out a breath of air.

'These jungle people know things,' he said. 'I thought these people were backward Indians living in the Stone Age. I thought these people were living behind the times. I thought they were uneducated and primitive because they don't have stuff, because they have not built stuff. No cars, no buildings, no big ships. No,' Russ said. 'These people, they know things. They know this earth, and they know the stars.'

I looked at Russ, who looked as if he had seen the answers to life's questions. 'What happened,' I asked.

'I inhaled this smoke,' Russ said, 'the breath of Pi's father and the smoke from that rock seemed to carry a knowledge from the dawn of time, and soon after it was like a fire hose blasted inside me, shooting out the top of my head, shooting a white light out the top of my head. It was a fantastic feeling. It was indescribable,' Russ said. Russ waved his hands in the air as he explained, 'mind blowing,' he said. 'I was this white light!'

'I was this light and I could see through it, and this light was spiralling up and out of my head. I was spiralling out the top of my head!'

Russ's mind, the mind of an engineer was working hard to explain as best he could such phenomena that cannot be explained through the boundaries of the material world. He blew out another breath and looked at me as if to say, 'try and stay with me.'

'We are this light,' Russ said, 'and this light is not sunlight. This is not firelight, it is a different light—it is an energy. It is the energy source of all things. It is the energy source from which matter is constructed.' Russ shuffled on the rock, finding a comfortable sitting position as he continued.

'I saw this light shooting out the top of my head and off it went, as far as the universe went. Off I went! I could see through it. I was it. I was this conscious energy that had simply been looking through the boundaries of the physical me.' Russ paused. 'And I am much more than the physical me.'

'And you!' Russ said pointing at me. He pointed at the trees and the river, he pointed in every direction. 'You and the trees and every living thing of this world have this life force running through us. I saw it,' Russ said. 'We are this energy. We all are. Every cell and microbe inside me that makes up my physical being are all a part of this light and their light is making up the larger light that is running through me and you and them and the rock at the bottom of the ocean are all connected through this energy. I saw it passing through everything. I saw everything was coming out of it. This entire world is connected. We are the same energy, and we are together a part of light that is going right through our planet.' Russ blew out a breath of air. 'Our planet is a living being,' Russ said.

'Our planet is as alive as the cells in our bodies. It is alive as me. It is as alive as the trees in the forest and the fish in the ocean and it is connected to the other planets. It is moving with them and they are moving together, a part of the same light and bigger physical entities.' Russ looked at me and then at Gary. We were both silent. Russ tapped a small stone to the rock we were sitting on and then cast it into the river.

'This energy is one being. It is us and I saw it. I saw this light,' Russ said. 'This energy can be connected from any part of itself to any part of itself, this light has an infinite possible points of connection and I saw every possible form of geometry I could fathom, like I was looking through a zillion kaleidoscopes at once. It is possible for this light energy to be manipulated into any form—and our mind is what gives it whatever form we wish for, consciousness is moulding it into shape. Into this incredibly complex three-dimensional imagery of a dense material world.'

'This light is consciousness, it is awareness and it finds a home through the boundaries it creates and perceives and we are nothing more than the consciousness of ourselves experiencing the embodiment of our self.'

I stared at Russ, never had I heard him speak like this before. I stared and I said nothing.

Russ blew out a deep breath and threw another stone into the river and we both gazed over the flowing water into the dense jungle on the other side.

This light that Russ spoke of. This energy that is us. It must be the love I felt. The world which Pi is in touch with. I stared at the river.

The river was mesmerizing and the night we had both had was deeply impacting. We sat in silence for a long time, listening to the sounds of the water washing against the riverbed. Listening to the sounds of the jungle. We sat, listening to the insects and the birds. We sat and listened until Gary spoke.

'They live hand in hand with the other worlds,' Gary said. 'They live with a real connection with this land; with the plants that grow from it and the animals that walk upon it. They have eyes in many worlds and can see interactions we have before they materialise.' Gary stood up looking at us both.

We both sat feeling like two birds in a cage, who only now realised the door was open, and that there was a world to explore. Gary sat back down and looked more comfortable as Russ stared at the moving water away in his thoughts.

I lay down and stretched out on the large warm rock. The sun had been heating it and I felt exceptionally comfortable. I closed my eyes and fell into the heat of the rock. I drifted away with the sounds of the river. I drifted easily into sleep.

I fell into a dream.

I fell into a dream unlike any other.

It was a dream unlike any other, and if I had not awoken, like most dreams, I would never have known that it was a dream.

10. The basic learning

I was with a girl and we walked as if I was on a journey to a new land that was only an idea that had never been discovered before. She was extraordinarily beautiful, with long blond hair, big dark blue eyes and a smile that shone stronger than any smile I had seen before.

Together we walked a mountain path. It was a long path and we had walked a long way. It was a steep path and the surrounding mountains were tall. In every direction tall rocky mountains with icy glaciers covering their tops reached high above the clouds. We walked the steep path until we arrived at a very old and very beautiful building. A huge old building alone in mountains, high above the clouds

In front of two large intricately carved wooden doors, stood a man. He was a similar height to myself, and somehow, he looked familiar. He was bald with a long white beard and he bore a large smile and through his glasses, his eyes were strong. His eyes were penetrating, as if he could see every detail of our skin. He leaned forward towards me.

'Welcome,' he said.

Then he waited, as if it were our turn to speak. I looked at him. I looked at the detailed carvings etched in the doors before which he stood.

'What is this place?' I asked.

The man followed my eyes; looking at the doors he was standing in front of and then back to me. He stepped aside making it clear he was no guard to its entrance, then gave me a look that suggested my question was something he could not answer.

'I can tell you what this place is for me, but how can I say what it will be like for you?' the old man replied.

'Would you like to come in?' he asked.

He opened the heavy wooden doors easily with one hand and as we followed he turned to us. 'This is,' he said, then he looked up and pondered for a moment, 'a school,' he said, 'and it will give you any teaching you ask for. It will give you every lesson you are ready for and you are free to stay as long as you wish.'

Then, he looked into the palm of his own hand, as if that was enough explanation for now.

I turned and looked around. Such a building—the huge windows that faced the view of the jagged mountains, the clouds that soared beneath us. Such detail. The detail in the window frames. The detail in the walls. The detail within the stonewalls was unlike any stone I had seen before.

I peered closely.

The walls were moving.

They seemed to be alive.

Moving walls like the inside of a thousand wristwatches. I peered closer still, so close I thought the wall would reach out and pull me inside. It was changing as I looked at it.

The movement of clockwork geometry within the stone took the form of an 'eye' and it opened. It blinked. I stared at the wall.

The stonewall looked back. Then the eye disappeared back into a movement of moving geometry.

It was aware of me.

I ran my finger across the stone, feeling its detailed movements press against my skin. It pressed gently, working its way over and around the lines of my fingerprint. Tiny fragments of stone running through the details of my fingerprint, searching every piece of my skin. Tiny pieces of clockwork stone.

Slowly the stone reached in. It reached into my skin, it reached into my mind, it reached in, gently like a caterpillar walking the lines of my skin. It was searching. Searching me. Searching my mind. I felt the walls. I felt what they are a part of, the walls that made up this old building.

This school was alive.

Alive and curious of me, the stranger who walked the mountain it sat on and stepped through its doors. I stood looking, captured by the wall of the school, my finger pressed softly against it.

Alive with the knowledge of stone, stone that has been from the beginning of time. Wisdom and knowledge was within these walls—I felt it. A knowledge older than time.

I released my finger and took a step back, I stood back staring at the wall. Complex geometric clockwork gears, tiny, moving together within the stone. I turned while looking around. The old man was gone. The girl I had come with was gone. I looked around the great room I was in. Great stone walls holding up huge high ceilings. Large windows stretched the length of the huge room I was in and they looked down to the clouds below and up to the rocky mountains above. I looked at the clouds floating below, I looked at the jagged mountaintops rising through them and I looked at the frames of the huge windows. They were as detailed and moving and alive as the walls.

I stood alone, as the timeless life that lives within the walls of the school crept in.

Creeping through the air, creeping through the walls, creeping from the mountains and into this school. This timeless life-force of knowledge crept in—it crept in and it spoke. It spoke slowly and it spoke clearly. A soft yet powerful voice. The gentle voice of a woman.

'All who come here choose to,' the woman's voice spoke, 'even if they do not know it, and all who come here will be given what they seek, even if they do not know what they are seeking.'

Her voice echoed through the building and through me and I felt the school. Every piece of every wall had its eyes on me. The ceiling, the floor, and the air in the room had its eyes on me, looking from every angle. The whole school had its eyes on me.

I stood looking over the clouds and up to the mountains when the large windows reaching from the floor to the ceiling burst open. They opened with a force and I felt a light breeze hit me, as I stared out at how high I was. The same soft voice spoke. She whispered softly through the walls, she whispered softly through the air that flowed in from the tops of the mountains.

'Wind,' she said.

'What you need is a little 'wind.'

As I heard these words a gush of wind burst through the large open windows. It picked me and threw me in the air, throwing me around and around until I hit hard against the wall behind me.

It pressed me high against the stonewall, wind pushing against me so hard I could not move.

I could not get down. I tried to push myself down but I could not. The wind was too strong. I tried with everything I had.

The woman's voice was soft and gentle as she spoke.

'You will get what you seek here,' she said.

'This wind is what you seek, but be warned, if you fight this wind then a fight is what you will have. This wind is not your enemy, yet it will give you what you seek.'

'Love,' she said.

'Love will set you free.'

Her words echoed through the wind, through the walls and through the mountains and the school. The word 'love' echoed through her whisper and seemed to cling to the fabric of the wind.

I opened my eyes and there I sat, in the middle of the room with my legs crossed and my back straight. I looked out the large open windows. There was no longer any wind, and the windows were no longer facing the mountains.

I walked to the edge of the large open windows. The school was no longer in the mountains.

I looked up and I looked down. The school was now in space. All I could see were stars and in front of me just below the windows ledge, but a few steps away, parked in mid space, was a spacecraft.

It was a round disk shape with a see-through dome top, with enough space to seat one person, and standing beside me was the old man with the long white beard. He looked at me and then turned to the spacecraft. I stood looking out at the stars.

His rested his hands on his hips and he let out a deep chuckle, a large smile stretched across his face.

He turned back to me, and through his glasses I saw he was searching my eyes. 'You found the ship,' the old man said.

He turned and gazed dreamily at the stars, a world he seemed familiar with, then he leaned forward towards me and peered close, as if to say, 'now what?' He glanced at the spaceship and again back to me.

'The ship was always here,' the old man said 'you just didn't see it before.' I looked at him trying to understand. He looked at me, then took a step behind me and pressed lightly on my temples.

'Look,' the old man said.

He pressed my temples and everything was light.

Me, the school and the space—everything was light. Nothing but light, and as he released a slight pressure the light dissipated bringing back into view the stars, the space, the spacecraft and myself. Except there was light left. The light that remained was a grid running through the stars. It was running through me and it was running through the old man. Every star connected on a grid of light, every star a part of a grid and for a moment I thought I was a star. The old man turned to me while pointing at the spacecraft.

'This ship travels with your thought,' he said. 'It travels the light and it will travel to the exact world you wish to go.'

I stepped onto the small spacecraft, opened the dome lid and sat inside. There was a round seat in the centre and I could turn and look in any direction. There were no controls, only a long low humming sound. Humming that had a pulse, humming that vibrated through the ship. It was not coming from the ship but rather it was everywhere. It was in me. It was running through me and as I listened closer, I heard how very complex it was. A low calm pulsating sound. This sound was a symphony of music. This sound was me, or rather I was it, or if I was sound then this is the sound that I would be. If this sound were physical, then I am this sound's physical form. The old man pointed to the ship and I looked at him through the dome lid.

'This craft resonates with you,' he said. 'It resonates with you and travels the light that connects the stars. It takes you through the light to the exact world you are resonating with. There are many worlds,' he said.

The old man smiled. 'There are infinite worlds,' he said, 'and remember, every world is a school and you will get what you seek.'

The sounds and vibration ran through me, and grew rapidly stronger. They ran through the spaceship and they ran through the light. The sound took me over. Only sound, the sounds of myself, the sounds of the spacecraft.

I travelled with the spacecraft.

I travelled as sound.

11. New living

I woke to a cool breeze from the river and the sun melting into my face. Gary was standing up. 'We must leave soon,' he said, 'it is important I am in Sao Luiz tonight.'

Gary's aircraft was small. There was enough room for Russ to stretch out in the back and for me to sit up front next to Gary. Both Russ and I left what belongings we had with Pi and his family. The idea was that our bags, shoes and clothes would become useful to them.

We moved away from the Sun as we headed for the Atlantic coast. Russ gazed at the jungle below and the large river that snaked its way through it as we reached our cruising altitude. I sat next to Gary wearing everything I had, shorts and a t-shirt, minus shoes. I held, and looked at, the necklace of threaded seeds Pi's father had hung around my neck before we had left.

'Dreams,' he had said, 'listen to your dreams.'

It was long and hung easily around my neck. Seeds of red, black, brown and green, every seed was different, different in shape and different in colour, yet they fit together snugly. I let it fall and rest on my chest. It felt good to wear. I felt a part of them was still with me. I looked down at the tree canopies below, gazing at the world that was their home.

'You wanna fly?'

I turned to Gary. He motioned for us to change seats. 'Fly the plane', I asked?

'Yes the plane,' Gary said, 'what else would you fly around here?'

Of course, I thought. 'Yes I wanna fly!' I said.

I moved over and sat in Gary's chair, my smile growing as Gary explained the controls. He chuckled, as he gave me what was undoubtedly the quickest flight training that had ever taken place.

He pointed to the throttle. 'Speed,' he said. He pointed to another control, 'this is the rudder, he said, 'left and right.' He gripped the stick which controlled accent and decent. 'The flaps on the wings make the plane go up and down.' he said. Gary rolled his eyes backward and forward while making an up and down movement with his hand—smiling and chuckling slightly.

I looked at Gary and laughed.

From where we were I could see the coast and Gary pointed to it. He pointed to the degrees on the compass and back to the coast. 'That's where we're going and we're good to get there,' he said. 'The weather is good and we can stay at this altitude and on this course until we descend. Gently,' Gary said. 'Gently move the rudders of the tail and wings and stay at this altitude.'

Gary shifted back the passenger seat of the plane, folded his arms and picked up a large straw hat from behind his seat and rested it over his eyes.

This man had just given me a two-minute flying lesson and now he was going to sleep! I looked to the back of the plane at Russ lounged into the small seat with his feet resting on some boxes, looking as comfortable as Gary.

There were very few clouds in the sky and the horizon grew slightly darker as the sun moved down in the west. I looked at the jungle below, I could only marvel at the river that moved through it. I slowly moved the rudder, feeling the plane turn easily to the left.

The plane turned opening up a new area of land to gaze upon. It was exhilarating.

I turned back to our course and then turned the plane to the right, bringing into view yet more of the land and vast jungle below. I pushed the stick controlling the pitch of the wings forward and the plane took a gentle dive. As the plane lunged forward we lost altitude and I watched the sudden change in perception. A slow and easy dive. I brought the aircraft back to our cruising altitude and headed for the horizon.

I felt good, I felt better than ever before. I felt clean and elastic. I felt new. I felt my hands as they held on to the control stick of the aircraft. They felt good. Every movement I made felt exceptionally good. My feet felt good. My hands felt good. Every movement felt unbelievable good. I laughed aloud—it is good to be me!

I pushed the stick harder forward, diving the plane towards the jungle below. Feeling the speed, seeing the jungle move fast underneath.

Exhilarating!

It is good to be me. It is good to be in my body and it is good to be flying. The plane dove steeper towards the treetops. I wanted to pull up at the last minute and feel the plane brush against the canopies. I wanted the plane to fall into a dive. The angle of the plane increased. I wanted to look vertically down. I wanted the plane to free-fall and I wanted my stomach to fall into my head. I pushed the stick further forward and the plane took a not so gentle sharp dive forward.

Russ and Gary both woke up. 'What the hell!' Russ said, shock filling his voice. Gary abruptly woke, shaking as he did, looking as he had just come from a cardiac arrest. 'Jesus Alexander!' Gary yelled. He pulled back the stick until the plane flattened out, taking us on a great swoop. He looked at me as though I had lost my mind and pointed to the Altimeter. 'Here!' he said. 'Jesus man, you want to be a burning wreck in those trees!?'

He stared at me, his face was full of surprise, but I saw the smile creeping through. It crept through and he smiled. He smiled because he loved to fly. He smiled because he may well have done the same thing being in my position.

However, flying was not the only exhilaration that was passing through me. I was indeed operating the plane, feeling its speed and manoeuvrability, yet I was also operating myself.

Not only was it fantastic to sit with my hands on the controls of the plane, feeling the controls within my grip. It was fantastic to feel the grip of my hands around the controls. I was not only operating the aircraft. I was operating myself. And I was hit with the fantastic feeling that it is, to be in the body that is mine.

Again we cruised at Gary's desired altitude and again Gary sat, slumped into the passenger seat with his eyes closed breathing soundly. I looked down at the earth we flew above. I laughed aloud—a big round Earth—such a concept for existence!

The sunset to the west reflected pink and orange in the windows of the plane. The sun, a big ball of fire and us, on this earth—we're moving around it. I looked down at our world. Me—this form that I am, this human form. Legs, arms and teeth. Eyes! Life could not be more brilliant.

I felt for the first time I was feeling myself; what I am; feeling the being that I am, what I am in control of. Me. I was not only flying the plane. I was flying myself, and I am even more excited to sit in than this plane. This body of mine. This instrument. This amazingly complex ship that is me.

Gary made some waking noises, and then lifted his straw hat from over his eyes while straightening up.

He looked to the horizon and he looked at the instrument panel. He looked at me. A sleepy smile was upon his face. 'Good,' he said, 'we are still in the air.' He threw his hat to the back of the plane where Russ was sleeping and we swapped seats as he put on and straightened his headset.

From the air I could see the city. It looked busy. I watched the surf rolling in from the Atlantic to the shore. After some talk on the radio Gary turned the plane inline with the runway and brought the plane down, and we landed as dusk was approaching.

Russ and I stepped out, our bare feet touching the tarmac. I had nothing with me, only shorts and a t-shirt, phone, passport and a bankcard. It was a warm evening and we perspired a little, the sounds of the river and birds were gone. The insects and the wind through the trees had been replaced with the noises of the city. No longer did I feel the earth under my feet but the all too familiar hard concrete. The smell in the air carried fumes from the aircrafts and the rest of the city that passed through my lungs. I turned to Russ.

'I want to go to the mountains,' I said.

But before Russ could respond, Gary who had not exited the plane opened and stuck his head through the cockpit window.

'I have to go,' he said. 'I must pick up a parcel and deliver it.' Gary started up the engine and the noise and wind from the propeller hit me. He put down his headset and hopped out the plane.

We, both Russ and I, hugged Gary and said goodbye to a man that had taken us to a place we had not expected to arrive at. We watched as he drove his plane to the far side of the runway. We watched as he hopped out and carried some parcels to his plane from a small hanger and we watched as he started his plane up again and lined up with others ready for take off.

Russ and I walked barefoot toward the large terminal of Sao Luiz.

12. Mystical

We walked through the sliding doors of the busy terminal, and before I could tell Russ my desire to climb a mountain, he told me he was going back to Norway.

You're going home?' I said staring at him.

Russ stared at me. 'It's Christmas tomorrow,' Russ said, 'I should to be with my kids and wife.'

"I want to climb a mountain,' I said.

Russ looked at me in disbelief. 'A mountain, you want to climb a mountain? Christ Alexander, it's Christmas tomorrow.'

Russ stared at me and I stared at Russ.

Together we were flying to Sao Paulo and from there Russ was connecting to Europe and I was flying to Lima, the pacific side of the continent, from where I could find my way to the Andes.

We walked to our gate and were happy to find the usual selection of boutique shops. Russ bought some warmer things as he was heading to the minus degrees of the north and I bought a pair of lightweight sand shoes and changed into new shorts and t-shirt.

The terminal was busy, and we had a few hours before our flight so we took some seats at the bar beside our gate.

The bar was busy and the bartender was constantly taking and making orders. Russ and I waited and we were about to order food when a large man pushed himself between us, throwing his money on the counter. I looked at Russ and Russ looked at me.

'Well I guess we are invisible,' I said.

Russ laughed unconcerned by the large man, or the fact we would have to wait a minute longer to place our order.

This large man looked as though he had spent every waking moment eating steroids and lifting trains. His eyes looked cloudy as if a conversation was taking place within himself and he had no time to listen to anything else. He ordered his drinks and turned to me.

'Have you something to say little man?' he asked.

I looked at him.

A stabbing pain shot through my stomach.

I felt ill and I looked away.

I looked down, my head in my lap. So incredibly ill.

The pain of this man shot through me. The pain of his world came crashing into mine. This man's poison came rushing into me and I felt it. I felt it inside me. His pain wanted a place to live. It wanted me to feed it. It wanted me to support it. It wanted me to recognise it. It wanted me to say, 'Yes, your pain is real and I will be a part of it.' It wanted me to stand up and hit this man's teeth into the back of his neck!

I raised my head and looked at this large man, feeling his pain, and then, I felt his pain pass through me. This man's pain entered—and then it left. I did not take it.

Russ sat staring at me as though he had seen a ghost.

Never had I felt another's pain pass through me like this. Never had I realised it had even entered. It had always stayed. It had always been invisible. I had always supported it. I had always supported it with my own pain. I would have jumped up and showed this man his pain was no match for mine, I would have cracked his teeth into his skull and broke his skull into the floor.

Russ stared at me, his eyes wide.

The man collected his drinks, carrying four glasses of beer balanced within his two large hands. He stepped away from the bar, and while looking into my eyes he smiled. 'That's what I thought,' he said, 'you have nothing to say.' The large man's smile was wide, then without noticing he turned and stepped into a young girl who waited to place her order. Avoiding spilling his drinks on her, he stepped to one side and lost balance, lunging towards us and throwing, what was some two litres of, beer over Russ and I.

Immediately I felt this man's beer soak through my shirt and run down my skin. Russ stood up looking at his new wet clothes with a face of utter discomfort. All but one glass the man was carrying had emptied and smashed on the floor.

I was wet with beer and this large man was angry, and he was angry with us. He poked me hard in the chest and I rocked back almost falling off the barstool. 'You two little fuckers sit here!' the man yelled. His eyes were filled with anger, an anger I was all too familiar with. I stared at him.

The pain that he was displaying, it did not come to me. I could not take it. I could not be a part of it. It didn't even touch me. This man's anger could not enter. There was nothing for it to interact with. I felt as calm as I had been when sitting by the river, and comfortable. I felt good to be in my skin, as good as I had when flying Gary's aeroplane. His anger did not affect me.

I looked into this man's eyes and all I could think was I wished he would drop his pain. I sat there staring at this large angry man. Then my mouth dropped open. It dropped when I saw them. I closed my eyes and opened them again. They were still there. I stared with my mouth open.

Standing by either side of this man was Pi and his father!

I stared in astonishment. They stood there, like spirit—ghost like as if they had just vibrated in from another world. They stood looking directly at me.

I heard them, I heard them as I had heard Pi speak without words—and they were laughing. They were laughing that my clothes were wet and that I had just bought them. They were laughing that I had no others and they were laughing that I was free from the poison that would have opened this man's skull and pushed every one of his glasses into his face. They were laughing at the situation I was in, and how coincidental it appeared to be. Their laughter hit me and I smiled. I laughed.

Pi and his father disappeared and this large man took a half beer that sat on the bar top and caste it in my face. 'You smile at me you little fuck! You laugh at me!' the man yelled. He shoved his fist in my face and pushed, I felt his knuckle's sink into my cheek. 'I will rip your mouth right off you face,' he said in my ear. He then thrust the empty glass into my stomach and left.

The entire terminal had been watching, and their eyes followed this large man as he walked away. I put the glass back on the bar.

People then turned their eyes on us, as Russ took off his new wet sweater and let it drop to the floor.

'I never thought I would see that,' Russ said.

'What?' I asked, 'Pi and his father?'

Russ looked at me, a puzzled expression on his face. 'No, that man. I never thought I would see you sit there and take abuse like that. He threw a drink in your face! Jesus man, you just sat there looking calm as if you were relaxing in the sauna. Something is wrong with you Alexander.' Russ smiled, and I could feel that for me not to react to this man was grounds enough for Russ to care nothing of the beer that soaked his clothes. Russ took off his wet t-shirt and threw it on the floor. He damped himself dry with some napkins from the bar and reached for a menu. He pointed to a sandwich, 'order me this,' he said, 'I am going to get more clothes.'

I called out before he left, 'get me the same as what I just bought,' I said. Russ turned back as he walked away. 'Shoes?' he asked. I felt my feet in my new sand shoes, they were comfortable and they were dry. 'Just shirt and shorts,' I called back.

Russ walked off and all who witnessed this large angry man yell and throw beer over me were now watching Russ. Their eyes were following him.

They watched him because he was a part of this scene. They watched him because he had no shirt on. They watched him because with the tattoo's that covered him, he looked like as gangster.

Not the street gangster sort, the sort that display scary eyes. No. The silent gangsters, the ones you don't know are there. The ones who hold pleasant conversations and wear expensive suits. The ones who never show their tattoos. Tattoo's you only see when they are forced to take off their clothes.

Yet Russ was no gangster, his tattoo's just made him look like one, at least to the population of this terminal. The population couldn't spot a real gangster if he were speaking on the TV, promising to give them what ever they wanted.

As Russ walked back to the boutique shop to buy the same clothes we had just purchased, people's eyes moved from him to me, as if they expected something more to happen. I ordered sandwiches and for the first time instead of ordering alcohol I ordered lemonade.

The young barman apologised for our misfortune and handed me some fresh dishcloths, informing me that our meals were on him. He turned to serve the young girl, the girl who this large man had stepped into.

I dropped the dishcloths I was holding.

It was her.

It was the girl from my dream.

It was exactly her. It was the girl I had walked with in the mountain. I stared at her—it was exactly her. She had the same hair, the same face, and the same body.

I stared in astonishment recapping the dream I had had.

She finished placing her order and turned to me, staring right at me as hard as I was staring at her.

'You saw them,' the girl said.

I stared at her, stuck for words. She spoke and I felt her, I felt her energy run through me.

The barman placed two lemonades on the counter and the girl took a barstool and sat next to me.

'Saw who,' I asked?

The girl smiled. She smiled a half smile and slightly raised one eyebrow.

I stared hard at her. 'You,' I said.

She looked surprised by my words. 'Me what?' the girl asked, her half smile turning into a full smile.

I stared. It was definitely her, that same shining smile. I said nothing.

'Me what?' she asked again, pointing her fingers towards herself.

What could I say to her? That I had dreamt we had walked to the top of a mountain. That we had come to a school and were met by an old man with a long white beard? I stared.

'You saw them too?' I asked.

The girl leaned closer keeping the conversation between us. 'Yes,' she said, turning and placing her hands right where Pi and his father had stood.

'You saw them?' I said.

She put down her teacup. 'Yes,' she said again, and before she could say more, Russ walked back to the bar. He was wearing a new shirt and carrying a bag containing my fresh clothes and he was walking with three men dressed in uniform.

Two of the men looked like they could be police and the other wore a neat plain suit. I stared at the men he was with, and all I could think was our blacked out trip down here was finally catching up with us. Russ did not look too phased by the men, however Russ was usually calm. He handed me my bag of clothes. People were staring again as one of the men in uniform interrupted the bartender from the order he was attending to.

The barman pointed to both Russ and I and to the girl beside me conveying the passing events between the large angry man and us.

I was relieved they were here to discuss this and looked into the bag Russ had given me to see the same clothes I was wearing. Russ took our sandwiches from the barman and placed one in front of me. Russ, unconcerned with the men in uniform began to eat.

I turned to the girl beside me. 'I'm Alexander,' I said holding my hand out. She shook it, 'Victoria' she said.

I took a sip from my glass and then left for the restroom to change.

I took the fresh clothes out from the bag and changed into them.

Still I felt sticky, but good to be dry. I put my wet clothes in the bag, then stuck my head under the faucet, letting the water run.

I thought of our flight to Sao Paulo. The water ran over my head and down my chest a little. These police were talking with people. Pi and his father were standing there and this girl had seen them too. I turned off the faucet and looked into the mirror. Russ was going back to Norway. I blew out a breath and dried my hair.

I was relieved to see that the men in uniform had gone and I sat back down next to the girl. I took a bite of my sandwich and before questioning her further I turned to Russ. 'What was that about?' I asked. Russ had a mouthful of food and did not stop chewing as he spoke. 'That man that threw beer on you is the son of a big shot politician,' Russ said.

Oh, I said?

'Yes,' Russ said, 'and the two police looking men are airport security and the man in the suit is some big shot that follows this guys son around, bailing him out of every mess he gets into.

He, wrote me a cheque,' Russ said.

'He wrote you a cheque?' I asked.

'Yes, the man in the suit wrote me a cheque,' Russ said pulling a folded piece of paper from his new shirt pocket. He handed it to me. I unfolded the cheque and looked at it. It was to the sum of two thousand dollars and the name was left blank. I laughed and threw it on the bar next to Russ.

'It's funny,' Russ said, through a mouth full of food. 'That big dumb man is lucky he didn't meet us when we were on our way down here.' Russ chuckled, staring at me with the same look of amazement.

The girl looked at me.

She looked at Russ. She looked at the cheque that lay on the bar top and the bag of clothes that lay on the floor.

'You have two sets of the same clothes?' she asked.

Her smile was beautiful. Her eyes were beautiful, and the way she looked at me brought me straight back to my dream. She poked inside with her eyes. Her question said more than just mere curiosity. She asked much more. I could feel it. I could see it in her eyes.

I stopped chewing.

I didn't know what to say. I didn't know where to start, she was asking me about me. She was not only asking why I had gone to change clothes only to come back wearing the same ones, she was searching through my eyes. She was searching like a child looking into a fish tank. Like a child staring at two hundred fish unable to see them all at the same time.

I said nothing.

'You two are incredible,' she said, looking at Russ and back to me.

She laughed aloud.

'Russ,' this is Victoria, I said, motioning toward the laughing girl who sat between us. I was going to mention we had started conversing over Pi and his father, but I did not.

Russ extended his arm and they shook hands.

As I finished my sandwich, Russ told Victoria of our work in the North Sea and how he was heading back to Norway. Victoria, glancing to me as she spoke told of her travels through South America and how she too was on her way home.

The final call for our flight was made and from where we sat we could see there were a few remaining passengers to board. I picked up my bag of beer covered clothes and looked at Victoria. I couldn't get the dream out of my mind.

'You saw those two men from the jungle?' I said.

Victoria slung her carry bag over her shoulder. She was also watching the final passengers board. I was glad to see we were on the same flight.

'Yes, I saw them,' she replied and as Russ and I headed towards our gate, she grabbed the cheque that Russ had left on the bar.

'You two monkeys gonna leave an unnamed cheque for two thousand dollars?' She waved it in the air and both Russ and I looked at it. Russ half smiled. 'Well it doesn't exactly cover our trip down here but it will buy us some new clothes,' he commented.

I laughed half-heartedly, both at the idea of being given a cheque so randomly and that here I stood boarding a plane wearing the same clothes I was carrying in a bag.

Victoria still held the cheque out between us. 'If you don't want it I'm happy to keep it,' she said. Russ took it and threw it in the bag I was carrying as if it was a receipt from groceries shopping.

We were the last to board the plane and the three of us sat together.

The plane took off and Russ closed his eyes, falling quickly asleep. I was also tired. I had not slept the previous night, but I was too interested in Victoria to sleep now.

'Those two men from the jungle,' I said, 'we stayed with them last night.' I pulled the long threaded necklace from under my shirt and showed it to her. 'They gave me this.' I took off the necklace and let it fall into her hands.

She looked at it closely.

I told her of the smoke and breath that had entered me. I told her of the world that seemed to connect us all. I told her of the pain I had spent hours choking on and the hours of vomiting that had taken place as this poison exited my body.

Victoria listened as she studied the necklace, 'wow' she said, a huge smile broadened across her face.

'Do you know who these people are,' she said. 'I thought they were different when I saw them.'

'This necklace is special,' Victoria said.

'It is?' I asked.

She handed the threaded necklace back to me.

'Why is it special?' I asked.

Victoria ordered two cups of tea as the flight host passed our seats.

She looked at me. 'Light, consciousness and matter,' she said.

I stared at her.

'Light is consciousness,' she said.

'This light, or this energy is one consciousness and it is observing itself. It is observing itself through matter. It is observing itself through the material objects that are here. You and me and your sleeping friend over there.'

She held up her teacup. 'And this, this teacup.' She held it down for me to look into, 'and the tea inside,' she said.

Victoria pointed at me. 'Your two friends, they know this and they travel the many realms of matter that we are a part of.'

'Matter?' I asked.

'How could they be matter? I could have put my hand right through them.'

'Not this matter,' Victoria said as she tapped her teaspoon to her china teacup, making a gentle ring.

'Yet matter nevertheless. They were travelling in a different body, a much lighter form of matter.

Realms of Spirit and Ghost. Realms that are dismissed by many. Realms that have their own natural laws and their own phenomena. Worlds of less dense matter. Matter that is still providing the boundaries for the one body of ourselves through which to perceive itself, and through which to interact with the very separate beings that we are.'

She poked me in the side of my stomach, jabbing her finger into me, wriggling it as if it were a worm.

'Pretty real hey,' she said. She smiled.

I smiled back. 'Yes, it's pretty real,' I replied.

Russ slept for the remainder of the flight and since I could not see how things could get anymore off the wall and since I would not see this girl again, I told her about my dream. I told her in detail from how we had walked up the mountain until I had stepped into the spacecraft and travelled with my own sound, only to wake up right by the river. I told her how the girl in my dream was the exact splitting image of her.

She stared at me.

She stared into my eyes. 'Ha,' she said and she half smiled.

She was carried away in her own thoughts for a few moments before she replied. She shrugged her shoulders, yet her eyes were searching, she was searching for something. 'Well I guess you are the spaceship she said, and you travelled to wake up right where you should be,' her smile broadened.

'But,' she said as she shuffled through her bag pulling out her travel documents, 'I won't be climbing any mountains as I am flying home from Lima tomorrow night.'

'You're flying to Lima?' I asked.

'Yes,' she said.

I pulled out my ticket. 'I am also flying to Lima.'

Victoria took the ticket from my hand and looked at it. 'Your flight is as soon as we land,' she said.

I looked at her.

'My flight is tomorrow morning,' she said.

Her eyes still searched mine and I wondered if she thought of changing her flight to mine as I thought of changing mine to hers.

The flight crew announced we were about to land and I looked out the window at the city lights of Sao Paulo.

We landed, exited the plane and looking at the time on the departure screen, I had to leave. I looked to see Russ was wearing a very similar necklace as mine. I pulled mine from under my shirt and Russ did the same. I looked back at the departure screen. I had to go. I turned to Victoria.

Her eyes were still searching mine. I did not want to say goodbye to her.

'You did not tell me what was special about this necklace,' I said. She just looked at me. She just stared at me and through her searching eyes I thought she looked almost teary.

I left Russ and Victoria with nothing but the clothes I was wearing and boarded my flight to Lima.

13. Lima

It was late when I arrived in Lima, and seeing it from the air I knew where I wanted to go. I didn't know the city and I didn't know the language but I knew the Pacific Ocean, and I knew there would be waves.

A man approached me with an ID card clipped to his loose fitting buttoned white shirt. He asked in good English where I was going and explained he was a registered airport taxi, or something to that effect. He looked eager for business. He looked eager like a man that did not get much, and my taxi fare was important to him. I was tired, yet excited with my new surroundings and pleased this man spoke English.

'I want to stay by the beach,' I said, 'where there are waves.' He was incredibly agreeable. 'No problem, he said, 'wherever you want to go I will take you. Where is your luggage?' the driver asked.

'I have no luggage,' I said as I closed the passenger door. 'I want to drive through the poorest areas of this city,' I said, 'and the wealthy. I want to see this city.' The driver's eagerness left and I watched his mind tick over before giving me a price in Peruvian sole. I pulled out the money I had—a fist full of Brazilian 'Real.' The driver looked at the crumpled notes. 'This is all I have,' I said straightening the notes slightly before giving them to him. His eyes widened.

Tired, I fell comfortably into the passenger seat of his car as the driver examined the foreign money, which was certainly overly sufficient, before looking pleased with the transaction. 'Where is your luggage?' he asked again. We drove away from the airport and I wondered where I had left my bag of beer soaked clothes.

I listened to the driver as we drove through the richer neighbourhoods of the city and the poorest. He told me about his family and life in Lima and Peru. I told him why I had no luggage. I told him how Russ and I had arrived in the Amazon and I told him of my plan to reach the Andes. I told him of the beautiful girl I would never see again.

It was late and dark as we drove along the coast, but the moon was big and I could see the waves were rolling in. Tall cliffs ran along the coast and above them facing the sea were apartments and hotels. 'There' I said pointing to the buildings facing the ocean, 'I want to stay there.'

The streets were busy and the night was alive with cafes and street food, but I had no feel to venture out. We stopped at a hotel facing the ocean and I checked into a spacious one-bedroom apartment.

Huge glass doors reached from the floor to the ceiling, which I opened letting a breeze from the ocean enter. I lounged into the reclining sofa chair and put my feet up. I sank heavily into the chair letting relaxation fill the room. I fell easily into sleep. I fell asleep with thoughts of surfing. I fell asleep with thoughts of the girl I had dreamt of and how I had then met her in the airport of Sao Luiz.

14. More surprises

I woke early to a chilled breeze coming in from the ocean that ran under my clothes and over my skin. I pushed myself up from the reclining chair and closed the sliding doors to the balcony. The breeze and the sounds of waves breaking stopped. I dropped my clothes on the floor and stepped into the shower. The large showerhead, as big as my head poured a stream of hot water over me. The large bathroom windows looked down to the surf and I stood watching the sets coming in.

Eager to get to the water, I dressed, slipped on my shoes and walked outside.

The fresh morning air of the coast was awakening and breakfast was fresh orange juice. I stood with a few others, who undoubtedly were here every morning, as an old woman with a wooden cart of fruit, pressed juice. I stood watching the waves from the cliff top. They looked good. I finished the last drop of juice, returned the glass to the woman and walked down to the beach.

The waves were gentle, occasionally over-head and they were breaking and peeling away smoothly. Tents lined the beach with a selection of different boards to choose from, and, as I approached, I saw how eager the owners of each tent were for my business. I walked towards the beach and passed a truck, in the back of which I noticed two beautifully shaped longboards. I looked at the waves. I looked at the boards in the back of the truck. I looked at the boards in front of the tents. This is what I wanted, one of these longboards would be perfect for these slow moving waves.

I walked to the tent that the truck belonged to, and held an imaginary sign that read, 'I am a customer.' A young dark skinned man dressed in all the fashionable surfing apparel rushed towards me, his muscular body painted in an array of tattoos that spoke of a lifetime in the water. He reminded me of a bad car salesman who doesn't care about selling cars, for he only wants to drive them. I was his brother and his friend and he told me how he loves my country, how my country has beautiful girls and how he has girlfriends from every country and how he has everything I need. How he has the right board for me— and on and on he spoke.

I stood listening to this man. I had said nothing as he continued talking. I only wanted the longboard in the back of his truck. I stood listening to him talk. I stood looking at him, listening to his mindless chatter. I stood listening to him chatter when I heard him. I heard what he was really saying.

I flashed back to my dream—when I was sitting in the spacecraft that travelled with sound.

Now. I was hearing him. I was hearing his sound.

It seemed to slide through an invisible crack from an invisible world.

I seemed to slide through an invisible crack, to a world where everything was sound.

I heard him and I heard myself.

I stood there listening to him talk of girls and parties in Lima and I heard his words, but I heard his sound. I heard the music that was playing within him. A symphony of sound that resonated him through the universe speaking a language of its own. A language I knew. A language we all knew. I heard it. I heard him.

I felt who he was resonating through me. I saw him. I saw why he covered his body in tattoos. I saw why he lifted weights and sculptured himself, why he strutted the beach in search of tourist girls. I saw why he dressed in the latest surfing apparel. I heard the sounds of the self underneath the tattoos and the surf brands. The symphony that he was. Such detailed melodic music. I felt as connected to him as I did to myself.

The sounds of this man—and the sounds of myself. I heard us both. My sounds and his sounds were playing together. Underneath our chatter we were playing music.

As we stood I listened to the music we were making. I saw the interaction we were having—an interaction of sound. My music and his music were playing together. I stared at him while I listened, and I almost forgot the longboard I was after.

My music.

His music.

We were playing ourselves. We were playing together.

I listened, and I chatted of the longboard in the back of his truck.

I smiled as we made brainless chatter. Brainless chatter disguised as fantastic music.

'This is my board, he said, and it is not usually for rent.'

'You may use it,' he said.

'Take a wetsuit,' the young man said.

I carried his board under my arm, excited to get into the water. 'No, I said it's warm enough.'

'Out here it is.' the young man said. 'Take a suit, if you don't you'll be out soon, take a suit and enjoy the waves.' I squeezed myself into a wetsuit. It was slightly too small, but no matter, I hurried to the surf.

This long light board was fast and effortless to paddle and I paddled out quickly to the back where the sets began.

I slid off the board and swam down. I swam deep and looked up. I exhaled, and watched the air from my lungs push through the water spiralling to the surface, air bubbles turning around each other as they reached for where they had come from. I looked through the dark cool water to the surfboard floating in the bright warm air above. It is good to be down, down in the cool ocean. Cold and salty water.

It was good to be in Lima.

Good people.

The taxi driver, the hotel staff, the lady making orange juice and the man who gave me this board. It was good to be here.

I floated to the surface and slid back on the board. Surfing—there is nothing that compares to it. To be in the elements. To be apart of the world that we live on and take advantage of such an occurrence as waves that break. Every time I'm in the surf I think about it. Such an occurrence—this earth—the form that I am—to ride waves of salt water. Such a combination of events that lead to something fantastic.

The board was brilliant. It manoeuvred like a board half its size and was easy to paddle out again after the long ride in. I was glad I was in Lima and after some time in the water I forgot about going to the mountains. I forgot that Russ had gone home and I forgot about the girl from my dream, and I did not leave the ocean until my muscles were tired and my stomach was pushing for food.

I bought a bag of fruit from a passing girl and took a seat on a rock, and with my wetsuit pulled down to my waist I watched the surf and felt my muscles rest. A wooden skewer stuck from a piece of fruit in my bag and I took it and held it up. I sat looking at the cubed fruit stuck on its tip, then I froze.

It was her.

I only saw her from behind as she zipped up her wet suit, yet I was certain it was her. Then she turned around, her eyes closed, the sun in her face as she tied her hair up. She turned again, her back to me and faced the sea. I swallowed the fruit in my month. She had not seen me, and as quickly as I spotted her, she grabbed her board, skipped into the surf and was paddling into the whitewash.

I sat staring. How could I see her again? I ate while watching her paddle, then zipped up my wetsuit and returned to the water. Funny, I thought. Funny to see her here.

I paddled out and sat next to her. She sat breathing heavily, resting her hands on her board.

'Hey,' I said.

She turned, 'You,' she said surprise filling her voice and as a wave moved underneath her she lost balance and rolled off her board splashing into the water. I looked at her treading water and she looked at me. 'What are you doing here?' she asked.

She was beautiful, the salt water soaking her hair and beading down here face, her big smile, her shining eyes.

She splashed me and slid back on her board. 'Are you stalking me?' she asked with a smile.

I couldn't believe I had dreamt of this girl. I couldn't believe she had seen Pi and his father. I couldn't believe I had sat next to her on our flight and I couldn't believe I was meeting her here.

'Yeah, I'm stalking you,' I said, 'I am a secret agent.'

'Oh,' she said, 'you're a secret agent are you?'

Victoria smiled. 'I thought you were just wandering with no idea of what you were doing,' she said. 'I thought you were just letting the world make decisions for you as you threw away your money every chance you got.' She raised one eyebrow. 'You fooled me,' she said.

'Yeah,' I said, 'that's my cover.'

'And you are definitely holding your cover well,' Victoria said, her eyes widening as she stretched her head forward toward me. 'A cheque for two thousand dollars,' Victoria said, 'remember?' Her eyes remained wide.

'What cheque?' I said.

She splashed me. 'Are you serious? A cheque for two thousand dollars sitting in a bag with a pair of your shorts and a shirt inside.'

She stared at me.

The bag with my clothes in it. I had left it and Russ had put that cheque in it. I was silent.

'You left it by my feet in Sao Paulo,' Victoria said.

I had forgotten about the cheque, but I was reminded that I needed new clothes as I had nothing and I thought about finding a shopping centre later.

'Hey! Are you listening?' Victoria waved her arm in front of me. 'Two thousand dollars! You walked off and left me standing with your friend, your friend walked off and I was left next to your bag with a huge cheque in it.' She splashed me again. 'And now your clothes and cheque are with my things at the airport.' Victoria raised both her eyebrows.

'Why are they there?' I asked.

'Because I'm flying home this afternoon, and I did not think I would see you here so I did not bring them,' Victoria said keeping her eyebrows raised.

I thought about the necklace. She had not said what was special about it. I thought of Pi and his father. How could I dream about someone, and then meet them—twice? I just looked at her.

Victoria laughed, dropping her eyebrows, she looked as if she had found something in my eyes.

'That's a nice board you found, Victoria said, 'shall we get some waves,' and our conversation ended as what was one of the larger waves I had seen that morning came breaking toward us. We both paddled to the left and were pushed along easily by its power. The both of us standing, riding the same wave to the shore.

The late morning went by and we got plenty of waves and I was glad I had taken a wetsuit.

Salty and tired, we sat on the rocks by the beach with our wetsuits pulled down, the sun drying our skin. We sat eating sliced fruit with wooden skewers from small plastic bags. I turned to Victoria. 'Tell me about the necklace they gave me.'

Victoria stuck the skewer into her bag of fruit—it stuck balancing from a large piece of mango. She swallowed as she held one hand to her mouth and one to my shoulder, 'that necklace is special,' she said 'and those men made it especially for you.' Victoria pulled the piece of mango from her bag and held the skewer in the air. The large piece of cubed fruit stuck to its end. She shuffled slightly.

'We are connected to the life inside us,' Victoria said. 'All the tiny pieces of life inside us, that together make our physical being, we are connected to.' Victoria leaned slightly forward and opened her eyes a little wider, 'they move separately from each other as individuals yet they make you your own whole being.' Victoria leaned back and let her eyes relax. 'And we,' Victoria said, 'are all connected to each other, even though there seems to be an awful lot of space between us.' A smile grew across Victoria's face. 'The stars are connected to each other and we are connected to the stars.' She placed the piece of mango in her mouth and stuck the skewer back in her bag and looked at me.'

She chewed slowly and then swallowed. 'You are your own unique set of connections to this world, which is different and unlike any other. The connections that you make. You have your own symphony of music that you are playing. We all do and no two symphonies are the same.'

Victoria pointed to the sky with the wooden skewer. 'We are connected to the stars and we are connected to the earth. We are connected to each other and all of our webs of connection are different. They are all unique as all of our sound is unique. We are connected to different people and different parts of the earth and we are connected to the stars—stars that are as different to each other as we are.'

Victoria poked me with the tip of the skewer and I felt it push gently to my wet suit.

'But although we are separate,' she said, 'although we all have our own world and we have our own physical person, we are not separate from each other. Our separate symphonies are playing together, just as the stars are all in the same sky.'

Victoria smiled. 'We are born from the stars.'

She put her bag of fruit down and looked at me. 'That string of seeds is uniquely yours and it is more than just a representation of the planets you are connected to.'

I stared at her.

She remained smiling and still she looked right at me. 'Everything has sound,' she said. 'Everything has vibration and each seed of that necklace carries within it a different vibrational sound. I heard them, and they are more than simply the vibrational code of the trees those seeds could grow into. Within each seed of that necklace is the vibration of other worlds. Other planets. The planets and the stars that you are connected to. They made that necklace for you, and for you alone.'

I stared at her.

'It's funny,' she said.

'What's funny,' I asked.

'I would never have known,' she said. 'I would have thought it to be just another necklace.'

'Never have known what,' I asked?

'I only noticed because I felt the vibration from one of the seeds. A planet I have been to before.'

I remained staring at her.

'You have been to another planet?' I said in disbelief.

'Don't look so surprised.' Victoria smiled, 'we're on a planet right now are we not?' She stood up and placed her empty plastic bag in the rubbish. She looked down at me. 'Some people are connected to the same stars, and after seeing your necklace I am not surprised we meet again.' Victoria did not sit back down. 'I have to go,' she said. 'You want your cheque and smelly clothes then you better come now.'

I stared at the sand between my toes then up at Victoria who was ready to go. 'Keep the cheque,' I said, 'I'm no secret agent, the real me is useless with money.'

'No,' Victoria replied, 'I won't keep it.' She threw me a towel she had brought. 'Dry yourself and come with me,' she said.

I put the towel beside me looking up at Victoria who was starting to look impatient. 'Keep the cheque,' I said, 'I don't care about it, it means nothing and besides it's not even mine, write your name on it.'

'I have to go,' Victoria said, 'I don't have time to argue with you. Dry yourself,' she said impatiently.

'Look,' I said, 'this necklace, this dream with you, the jungle, Pi and his father, planets and sound. I don't care about the money,' I said.

A taxi was waiting for Victoria to enter. She threw her arms around me and kissed me lightly on the cheek before letting go.

'Me too,' she said as she stepped into the taxi.

'You what?' I asked as she closed the door.

'Me too. I have not met someone like you,' she said, 'and me too I wish we were surfing again tomorrow.'

She blew a friendly kiss from the taxi as it took off and I stood there looking at where the taxi had been parked. I stood there with my wetsuit pulled down holding a half bag of fruit.

15. Victoria

Hot water bounced from my skin washing away the salt. I looked at the ocean through the windows that were beginning to fog—there were now more boards in the water. My clothes lay on the tiled floor, the same clothes that Victoria had at the airport.

Perhaps I should have gone with her?

I turned off the water and cracked open the window, the fog spreading over the mirror and glass began to clear.

I picked up the necklace and looked at it. It looked like seeds strung together. I thought of what Victoria had said and hung it around my neck. It felt good to wear. I dressed and walked to reception.

I took directions to a shopping centre and followed the cliffs to get a bag and some clothes. The cliffs were high and the path winding along its top moved around tailored flowerbeds and grassy areas for children to play. People were jogging and walking their dogs. Security guards were spaced out along the path of this wealthy part of Lima, snaking around manicured gardens and public exercise equipment, a notable difference from the poorer areas I had seen while driving from the airport. The hot sun was melting into my skin.

The shopping mall was big. It housed the same shops that had the same brands that were throughout Norway, and every other country I had been to. Boutique stores lined up one after the other. Women in high heels with manicured hair walked by either side of me. Men with tight-buttoned shirts and equally manicured hair walked with them. I looked around. My stomach tightened.

What factories had made these people? Every one of them was the same, pressed from the same mould, dressed with different accessories. They had the same factories here that they had in Norway. My stomach tightened further.

I wanted to leave. I wanted to leave and walk along the cliffs. I wanted to go back to the ocean and leave the pressed fashion that surrounded me. I wanted to leave but I needed clothes, I needed underwear and I needed a toothbrush.

I sat on the cliff top outside the mall, surrounded by the parading of people and looked at the ocean. I watched the surf coming in and the people in the water. I thought of the man I had rented the board from. Such music that came from him. Under the fashion of tattoos stamped over his skin, were such melodic sounds. I looked around. I could not hear these people. I could only feel my stomach tighten.

I sat for a long time watching the waves. I sat in my own thoughts until my stomach began to loosen. I wanted to go to the mountains. I thought of the tall mountains and the open space, just me and the mountains. I left the shopping complex and continued to walk, following the path that followed the cliff top. I walked for several hours until the path stopped. The cliff continued but the path along it with gourmet gardens of colourful flowerbeds ended. It ended, as did the condominiums and apartments, as this wealthy suburb moved into that of a poorer area, there was no longer a pleasant garden-filled path to follow.

I sat where the path ended and watched the ocean. I watched the surf as the sun moved towards the horizon. I sat until the sun touched the horizon and dipped below the ocean and It wasn't until I felt the chill in the air when the sun was gone that I walked back to the shopping complex.

I shopped fast. I bought a bag, which I filled with clothes and some toiletries. It was light and I slung the bag over my shoulder and walked back along the cliffs to my hotel. I walked up to the entrance of my hotel, only to pause when I saw the same taxi driver who had dropped me off the previous night. He was pulling luggage from the trunk.

This must be where he takes customers and I suspected he got something for the delivery. I crossed the street ready to greet this man.

Victoria stepped out of the car.

The taxi driver stood looking at me with a grin, a sense of accomplishment filled his eyes. I stood looking at them both and as he took Victoria's luggage from the trunk of his car Victoria saw me, and a smile broadened across her face.

I looked at her. Why was she here?

She had not taken her flight and she has found where I stay.

She thinks we are connected to the stars. Of course, I thought, I let her keep a cheque for two thousand dollars and now she is here. Now she is here with her luggage, smiling at me.

Crap, I thought, this is not good.

I crossed the street. 'What happened?' I asked.

Victoria exhaled of breath and tugged on my shirt. 'New clothes?' she commented.

'Yes,' I said, 'but what happened, were you not flying home, and now my taxi driver?' I pointed to the driver who was stacking

Victoria's luggage by the hotel door. 'And here?'

She tugged on my shirt and looked at my new pants. She smiled. 'They look good,' she said.

This is not good I thought, I just want to go to the mountains. I looked at her. She is so beautiful.

I did not want to think about clothes, or shopping, yet I could not hide my smile. 'Thanks,' I said. I grabbed each sleeve of her shirt between my thumb and forefinger and shook, making a wave of ripples run down her chest and stomach. 'What are you doing here?' I asked again.

Victoria laughed, yet blew out a longer exhale of breath. 'I lost my travel case,' she said. 'Bankcard, cash and Passport, all that stuff.'

'Oh?' I said.

The Taxi driver who was talking with the hotel staff came over to us. We shook hands, and he asked how I was enjoying Lima. 'Yes' I said. 'I like it, I like it here, but you are here with her?' I said.

The driver began laughing. 'It's funny,' he said. 'This is funny for these things do not happen everyday.' He placed one hand on Victoria's shoulder and spoke to her in Spanish.

Victoria smiled. 'Yes, I know you're not laughing at me,' Victoria said, prodding him in the stomach.

'I'm looking for customers,' the driver said. 'I need to drive people. I need to make business, same like always.' The taxi driver looked at me, his hand resting on Victoria's shoulder as he spoke. 'I see this young lady, she says she does not want a taxi, she explained she has lost everything. This is Peru, I told her, no one is going hungry here.

Everything is going to be fine, I told her. I was going to help her fix everything.'

'She told me she didn't know why she had lost her things.'

'I told her, that these things happen and not to worry.'

She told me she was not worried, she just wasn't sure why she had lost them.'

'She told me she had just left the airport today to go surfing, just for the day.'

I was going to take her to my friend's hotel where she could stay and pay later. Then I remembered you.'

The driver pointed at me.

'You are the Norwegian man she told me she met at the beach.' The driver smiled. His smile was huge, stretching across his face pushing his eyes to his forehead, showing his age with the wrinkles displayed. 'I don't forget if someone pays double with money from Brazil,' he said.

I stared at them.

I looked at his old car.

I looked at the hotel lobby.

I looked at Victoria and I looked to the ocean, I thought about the necklace around my neck. Perhaps we really were connected to the same stars?

'I have to go,' the driver said.

I stared at this man as Victoria exchanged some words with him in Spanish. 'No,' the driver said stepping into his car. Victoria turned to me. 'Can I have some money?' she asked, 'I want to pay him.'

I took what notes I had which was perhaps several hundred dollars as I had pressed the largest amount when withdrawing.

If this man was connected to me, or my, or Victoria's stars then this was the least payment that he should get. I leaned through the car window sticking my hand out.

'Are you giving free rides now?' I asked.

He could not grip around my hand to shake it for the stack of notes in my palm. He stared at me. 'You already paid for this fare,' he replied. He looked at the stack of notes in his hand. 'Do you know how much this is?' the driver asked.

I looked at him.

'Honestly, no,' I said, 'and don't tell me because I'll either take it back or give you more.' I stood back and he leaned forward to the window. 'I can buy a car with this money,' he said. I looked at the old car he was driving. 'Well don't do that,' I said, 'you already have a car.'

He handed me his card and said to call if we needed anything.

'You're keeping your disguise well,' Victoria said, 'lost traveller throwing money around,' she raised one eyebrow.

'Yes, I am no secret agent, and you,' I said, 'appear not to be stalking me.'

Stalking you?' Victoria replied. 'No, I am certainly not stalking you,' she said, as we walked through the hotel lobby.

I turned as we entered, 'you had that cheque you know.'

Victoria paused and looked as if she was trying to figure out why she had not remembered money when she thought she had none.

'I forgot about the cheque,' she said, 'and I have your clothes too,' she said, opening her bag.

Victoria stopped rummaging through her bag and looked at me. She looked as if she had forgotten to ask.

'Can I stay here?' she asked.

I looked at her bag, the stale beer odour drifted out from my clothes.

The driver was right. It was funny that she was here. It was funny that we meet again.

'Yes, you can stay here,' I said, while looking at her luggage. 'Of course you can.'

16. Past and present lives

'Excuse me Sir.'

I threw my thoughts to the side and glanced at the young woman at reception, but my eyes were like magnets and quickly moved again to the large fish tank behind her. So many colourful fish were swimming slowly around. I thought about the huge ocean they were taken from and I thought about the tank these fish were in. Such a small amount of water for these fish to spend their lives in. I looked at the size of this fish tank. This fish tank was big.

'Sir!'

'Yes, sorry,' I looked back at the receptionist.

'Your driver told me what had happened sir.'

The young woman handed Victoria a piece of paper and a pen. 'Please write what you are missing,' the woman said, 'I will call the airport.'

'Thank you,' Victoria said as she took the pen. I looked back to the fish tank.

The young woman placed another key on the counter and explained to Victoria the breakfast times, and that there was a swimming pool through the back courtyard. 'There is a swimming pool?' I asked. 'Yes sir,' the woman said and she explained directions to the pool.

A smartly dressed man loaded Victoria's bag onto a trolley along with some extra towels and I was about to follow, when I was caught by a large laminated photo of the woman at the desk by the ruins of Machu Picchu. The mountains were huge and clouds hung casually under their tops and the woman at the desk wore a huge smile. The woman pointed at the photo. 'Machu Picchu,' she said.

'It's nice,' I said.

'Yes,' she said, 'it's beautiful. I went there on my vacation,' she explained, 'with my sister and mother. It is very beautiful there,' she said 'and while you are in Peru, you must go there.' The woman smiled.

I looked at the picture. I wanted to go to these mountains. We left and thanked the woman as she picked up the phone to call the airport.

The porter left Victoria's bag by the door. A vase of flowers and a bowl of fruit sat on the counter top in my apartment that had not been there earlier. I opened the sliding door to the balcony and let some air into the room. Victoria chuckled with half a smile. 'Are you sure you're not a secret agent?' she said.

'I'm pretty sure,' I said.

She turned around while looking up, then walked through the sitting room and out to the balcony. She paused, looking at the view then walked across the balcony, and I heard the sliding of the door as she entered the sleeping room. 'Wow' she called out from the other room, 'this place has strong energy!' She came back to the kitchen as I was looking through a selection of teas. I looked at her.

She stood as if feeling every piece of the air. 'There is a presence here,' she said. I picked two teas and pressed the jug to boil, looking at her as she was captured by whatever it was that was in this room. I thought about Pi and hi father as I put two tea bags into two cups. 'Is it them?' I asked.

'No,' she said turning to me, 'this is not them.' I stood looking at her, letting the jug whistle. 'Are you going to stop that?' she said. 'Stop what?' I asked.

'The jug, it's screaming,' she said.

I reached over and took the jug, filled the two cups and handed one to her.

'They're here,' she said. 'Your friends from the jungle, they're here and they're watching but this is not them. This presence is not watching, it is filling this room and he wants you to listen.'

I put down my teacup.

'You are listening, that is why he's here.' Victoria chuckled. 'He goes where he's listened to.' She stood there looking in the opposite direction as me while feeling the room. 'He goes where he's listened to,' she said again, 'and he stays where he feels at home. He feels at home where he feels connected and he feels connected when you hear him. When you listen to him,' she said.

I picked up my tea and took a sip. It was too hot and I put it back down. 'I'm not listening to anyone' I said, 'and I don't hear anyone.' I blew on my tea and watched it ripple.

Victoria began laughing, a deep laughter as if she was laughing with someone. 'Yes,' she said, 'yes, that's funny,' then she turned to me. 'You don't even know you're listening, you don't even know what you're hearing.'

I said nothing and checked if my tea had cooled down but it was still too hot.

Victoria looked at me.

'This energy is filling this room and it's not going anywhere. It is pushing from you the pinnacle of what you wish to become. You have asked for this and they are listening to you. They have always been listening to you and now whether you know it or not you are starting to listen to them.'

I stared at my hot cup of tea and was about to take a sip when the phone rang.

'I have good news for you sir.'

It was the woman from reception. 'You do?' I replied.

'Yes sir, your wife.' I interrupted her. 'She is not my wife,' I said. 'Sorry sir,' the woman replied. 'Your girlfriend, sir.'

'She is not my girlfriend,' I said.

'Well your friend sir, it does not matter, the young woman, Victoria that is staying with you. They have her belongings at the airport.'

'They do?' I said.

'Yes, a young man found them on the floor and returned them. Her Passport and everything is there sir. Please tell her I am happy they have found her things, and if you need anything more please contact me.'

'Thank you,' I said.

'This is our pleasure sir' she said, 'we are happy you are staying with us.'

I hung up the phone.

Victoria's voice echoed from the other room, 'your bathroom is huge,' she called, 'it looks right to the sea!' She walked back into the sitting room and I took a sip from my tea, which was now pleasant to drink. 'How much do you pay for this place?' she asked. 'You stay in a fancy apartment and you throw money at taxi drivers and large cheques away.' She raised an eyebrow. 'Are you sure you're a fisherman?

Victoria opened her luggage and took out the plastic bag I had left in Sao Paulo. It smelt rotten and the smell had seeped through the rest of her things. She placed the cheque on the table.

'Well I wont argue with you about that again,' I said 'and if you say there's a presence in this room, it's not just looking out for me because someone turned your travel bag in to lost property at the airport.'

'No,' Victoria replied, her eyes widening. 'Are you kidding me?'

'Yes,' I said, 'I mean, no, no I'm not kidding you and yes, your bag is at the airport. She just called,' I said, 'the woman from reception just said so.'

Victoria put down her tea. 'Brilliant,' she said, 'I will go there now.'

I handed Victoria the taxi driver's card, 'get him to deliver it,' I said.

'Yes,' Victoria said, 'excellent.'

I handed her a key to the room.

'Why do I need this?' she asked. 'Where are you going?' 'Nowhere,' I said, 'I'm having a shower.'

'Thank you,' Victoria said as she closed the door and went to see the woman at reception.

I kicked the bag of smelly beer clothes through the door to the balcony. They stink and they can stay out there. I drank the rest of my now cold tea and threw the china cup on the sofa and watched it bounce a few times before resting.

I liked my bathroom, the showerhead was huge and the falling water hit every part of my skin. The sun had long since passed the horizon and I watched as one man surfed in the light of the moon. I watched him paddle and take a few waves until steam filled the bathroom and fogged the windows. I closed my eyes and felt the hot water. It was hot enough to burn but not hot enough to scald. I thought about the mountains and I thought about Victoria. Strange that she was here. I thought about the presence that she spoke of and I wondered when she would fly home now she had her passport back. A few weeks I thought, I was due back to the ship in just a few weeks.

I kicked the door to the bathroom ajar and watched the steam leave the windows. The ocean came back into view, and the moon moving further across the sky reflected enough light for the lone surfer to continue. I dried myself as I heard Victoria talking and then hang up the phone.

I picked up the teacup from the sofa and placed it on the counter top. 'Everything good,' I asked. 'Yeah it's good,' she said, 'the driver is going to drop my things off tonight.'

'That's excellent,' I said, 'so that was him on the phone?'

'That was the airline,' Victoria said, taking the teacup and placing it in the sink. She paused, and looked at me with her hands placed on the counter top. 'When are you going to the Andes?' she asked. I looked at her. Her eyes were searching. 'I don't know,' I replied.

'When are you flying home,' I asked?

Victoria looked at me. 'I don't know,' she said.

She looked at her luggage on the floor and she looked at the sky that was now becoming lighter with the moon rather than the sun.

We stood on the Balcony watching the one board in the water. Victoria leaned into the balustrade looking toward the sea. 'I want to go to Machu Picchu,' she said. She turned around facing me. 'I want to go to the school in the mountains. I want to go to the school from your dreams and I want to meet that old man. I want to go there,' she said, smiling 'and I want to fly a spaceship.' She chuckled a little and turned back to the moonlit ocean, her eyes following the surfer. 'I want to surf tomorrow,' she said.

He had a nice style.

His turns were smooth and he spent as much time standing up as he did paddling. We watched as he took his last wave of the night, and then carried his board up the beach.

Victoria pushed herself away from the balustrade. She stood and looked into my eyes. But her eyes were not searching. They were fixed on something. She had looked at me in a similar way before, like she was looking into a fish tank, looking at many different moving things, but now her eyes were fixed. She looked as though she had found one particular fish and she was looking right at it.

'I can see you, she said.'

I looked at her. My eyes were searching.

'I see who you are,' she said.

I watched as her eyes began to swell and a tear formed then rolled down her cheek. She remained fixed within my eyes, staring, as another tear peeled away.

She grabbed me by the arm, 'come,' she said, as she took me through the sliding door to the bedroom. 'Sit down' she said pointing to the bed, 'I want to show you something.'

Victoria sat with her legs crossed and I slid off my shoes and sat in front of her. Facing each other, we both sat cross-legged on the large bed.

Victoria looked into my eyes, her eyes fixed, fixed on something. 'Look,' she said, 'look into me, look and see what you see.' She placed her hands in mine. 'Look into my eyes,' she said.

Her hands were soft and warm and I looked into her eyes and I did not look away. I looked into her eyes, her big blue eyes. They began to swell and I watched as the tears that grew made large droplets, peeling away from her eyes and rolling down her cheeks. Her mouth opened slightly, more tears formed and more ran down her face. She breathed heavily and said nothing, her eyes fixed in mine.

I squeezed her hands and leaned forward. 'What's wrong?' I asked.

Her eyes flinched, and her gaze drifted from deep in my eyes to my face. The swelling in her eyes stopped and she squeezed my hands back. 'Nothing is wrong Alexander, these are tears of realizing,' she said, 'just look.' She shook my hands and looked back in my eyes with the same steady focus, again her mouth dropped and she stared into me.

I stared back.

Never had I sat with someone like this, I shuffled on the bed and looked at her.

A short time passed, and I turned and looked out to the ocean, the darkness of the ocean and the light of the moon, but with one finger pressed against my chin, Victoria returned my face to hers. 'Look into my eyes,' she said, 'and see what you see. Don't stop until you see.' Again she rested her hands in mine.

I looked into her eyes and I forgot about the ocean.

I looked into her eyes and I forgot about the mountains.

I looked into her eyes and I forgot about how soon it was until I would be back on the ship. I just looked.

Time passed and I stared.

I stared.

I stared and I saw.

I saw why she had told me to look. I saw why she told me to keep looking. I saw why she had pushed my face back to hers. My mouth dropped open in astonishment. My eyes widened and my heart sank deep into my chest. My eyes swelled.

Extraordinary.

Right in front of me. Right before my eyes.

She changed.

The colour of her skin changed from a tan white to dark black. Her long blond hair was gone and was now but a centimetre long. Curly and black. Jet-black hair, with big brown eyes, and her face had completely changed. This person in front of me was a completely different person. She was no longer a blue eyed blond girl in her twenty's. This girl I looked at now was a very young girl. A black girl. She was a child.

This child stared at me. Her skin was so dark. So shiny. So beautiful. This child was shining. She shone like she had just stepped from the clearest lagoon in the most beautiful jungle. Water beading off her strong healthy skin, with big beautiful clear, clean eyes that sparkled with happiness. Such a beautiful child.

I stared in astonishment.

Then.

As if watching a film on fast-forward, she grew. She grew older, and as she grew her facial expression changed. Her skin colour changed from dark shiny black to light brown. She was covered with sores. She reeked of sickness, so unhealthy and she no longer shone of happiness. I watched as her demeanour changed, as this child grew into a woman and as I watched I listened, to a dialogue that passed through me.

The life of this child. The life of this woman, who she was and where she came from, what had happened to her and what had caused her demeanour to change. I watched and my mouth dropped, the blood ran out of my head and my heart sank deep into my chest. My eyes swelled and tears instantly formed, tears pushed out by more tears and I choked on the horror of what I saw. I looked away, my face red and wet. I could not look anymore.

I looked back at Victoria.

There she sat. Victoria. The same blue eyed girl with long blond hair.

I let out a huge breath. Unbelievable.

She let go of my hands, and let out an equally huge breath of air. Shaken.

I was shaken.

She placed her hands on my chest while staring at me, her eyes swollen and red.

'You were black,' I said.

'You were a young black girl.' I took her hands from my chest and held them by our feet and explained what I saw. I could not hold my tears, I could not hold them back and as I let them fall, I spoke through them.

'You were so beautiful,' I said.

'My sister, you were my sister and we lived in paradise. We were so happy and you were so alive, so happy and so strong. Everything was perfect. It was so beautiful there.'

'Then men came.'

'Men came to where we lived. They killed so many of us. There was so much blood. They set fire to our village and they took you away. They took me away.'

'I saw what happened after they took you away, I saw what happened until you died as a woman.'

I could not say what I saw. It was too horrible. Too much pain.

I covered my mouth while looking at her. What pain she had gone through. A slave. A doormat. Spat on for the pleasure of men.

Victoria's eyes were drying. 'You were my brother,' she said. 'You were my younger brother and we lived in a village in middle east Africa. It was beautiful there,' she said, 'it was so very beautiful.'

'We lived with the land and we lived with the animals on it. We lived with our family and we lived with our village. 'We lived under the stars and we lived with them, and the water pools we swam in were ours and the land loved us as we loved the land.'

'Then those men came.'

'They destroyed our village. They killed the old, they killed the young who fought them, and they took everyone else.'

'They raped the women and took the children and they burnt the village, leaving nothing.'

'I watched them take you away and I could do nothing.'

'I watched them kill our family and I could do nothing. I never saw you again.'

Victoria let release a long breath wrapping her arms around me and resting her head to my shoulder.

We sat with each other in silence.

I was shaken.

I was completely shaken.

We sat in silence looking at each other. We just sat there on that bed looking at each other. We sat there until the phone rang.

I looked at this blonde girl with blue eyes.

Other lives I thought. Whole other lives, I fell back to the bed with my arms spread out staring at the ceiling. I stared at the ceiling thinking of this other life I had lived and what used to be my home.

The phone continued to ring.

I thought of the life I was living now. I thought of what life I might live in the future. I rolled over and sat on the edge of the bed— reaching I picked up the receiver on the nightstand. It was the woman from reception—Victoria's things had arrived. I hung up the phone.

Other lives, I thought.

Whole other lives.

Other lives that I had lived.

17. The secret window

We left our laundry with reception and while the woman behind the desk circled restaurants on a paper map, Victoria looked through her travel bag, 'It's all here,' she said.

I looked away from the map to the case containing Victoria's passport and money. She flicked her fingers through it. There was Euro, Swedish krona and currency I had not seen before.

She leaned over the counter, and as best she could, hugged the woman.

The woman blushed.

'We are happy you have your belongings miss.' She circled another spot on the map and pointed to it. 'This is Peruvian food,' she said. 'It is my favourite restaurant in Lima, it is cheap and it is delicious,' she said.

We took the map and walked away from the cliffs to the busy square of town.

The food was simple and fresh and as I finished the last of my fruit juice, I leaned into the comfortable plastic chair. The night air was warm and my stomach was full. I closed my eyes, listening to Victoria chat to our neighbouring table and I did not fight the sleep passing over me.

I placed my arms on my head as sleep began to move. I thought about getting up with the sun and taking the same board I had used this day. I thought about the mountains and the open space, the fresh air that was there and as I thought of Victoria as a young black girl, and as the sounds of the restaurant melted into the sounds of my mind, they swam together and I drifted comfortably away.

'You going to sleep here?' Victoria scratched my head.

I opened my eyes. I was in the restaurant, it was busy and Victoria was looking down at me. 'Come on, let's go,' she said.

I pushed myself out of the chair and the man at the table beside us wished me a good time in Peru, and said how beautiful the Andes were. Victoria waved goodbye to them and we walked back to the cliffs. The walk woke me up slightly, yet still, I felt tired and delightfully sleepy.

'Cocaina. Cocaina.'

A young man somewhat taller than Victoria jogged to catch up with us. 'Hey tourist. Hey! You want coka?'

I turned and looked at this man. He was not smartly dressed and he looked desperate to get rid of the stuff that he had. Before I had said anything he opened a folded piece of paper revealing a rock the size of my thumb. 'Here,' he handed it to me then looked around quickly and then back to me. 'Taste it,' he said, 'taste it.'

Victoria stared at me as I looked at this crystal rock in my hand. It was big and I stared at it.

It slipped through my hand.

I dropped it.

I dropped it and the cocaine hit the ground and the crystallized rock broke and scattered on the pavement, the paper blowing slightly with the wind.

Pi and his father!

Pi and his father stood staring at me. They stood like strong tree trunks on either side of this man. I stared at them. I stared at this young man as he watched his cocaine hit the pavement and blow away with the wind. This young man stared at me, forgetting his English cursing my stupidity in Spanish.

I stared at Pi and his father.

His words hit me—they hit me hard as I flashed and revisited my night in the jungle. The night in the jungle hit me hard. The screaming hit me hard. The crying hit me hard and the taste of the poison I had spent hours vomiting filled my body.

'No more poison,' Pi said, 'no more poison.'

Victoria handed the young man some money and after a short spurt of Spanish she pushed me forward and I stepped right where Pi was standing.

I stepped right through Pi and I felt him as I did. I felt him fill me, I felt him push and fill every corner of who I am. I felt again who he was. I felt him fill me and I felt the same love I had felt in the Amazon.

'Love,' he said, 'love.'

'No more poison.'

I looked back but Pi was gone and all I could see was the young man hurrying away, then turn down a side street.

We walked to the cliffs. We crossed the barrier that ran along the neat path and sat on the edge of a rock with our feet hanging over the side.

We were high and the breeze and sounds from the ocean filled the air.

I turned facing Victoria. 'Did you see them?'

She smiled, poking me in the leg. 'They like you,' she said.

She had not taken her finger from my leg and she poked me again. 'They are looking out for you.'

I looked at her. 'Is that why they're showing up, they want to stop me fighting and filling my body with poison?' I looked at her finger resting on my leg, waiting for her to poke me again.

'I was not going to taste it,' I said, 'I was just staring at it thinking how I had been controlled by that world. When I saw Pi and his father I dropped it.'

Victoria looked at me.

'They don't stay around you because they are trying to stop you from fighting and filling your body with poison,' she said. 'They stay around you because you are stopping. They are not trying to push you into their world. They are accepting you because you wish to enter it.' She released her finger from my leg and pointed to a small blue flower poking out from a bush. It stood alone and its colour lit up with the light of the moon. It was a silhouette in the night sky hanging over the cliffs edge.

'That flower,' Victoria said, 'is always there.' Victoria pointed to a bird sitting on a branch a little further away. It sat as still as the flower. I looked at the bird and I looked at the flower, both of them shining in the light of the moon. Such colour in the bird's feathers, such colour in the flowers petals. 'They are always there,' Victoria said.

'You can tell the busy man, on his way to work, to look at that flower. Look how beautiful it is and look at the bird, see how colourful it is and the man will see it. He will see it and he will wonder why he never noticed them before since he walks this path everyday. He will then walk to work, and he will walk past and he will not see, a hundred flowers and a hundred birds of equal colour and equal beauty.'

'You cannot make someone see the world around them, as Pi and his father cannot make you see them. The presence that is surrounding you and filling your hotel room cannot make you listen. Yet it is there,' Victoria said, pointing at the flower hanging over the cliff. 'It is always there and the sounds that run through the universe and through us are always there. The world of spirit is always there.'

'That stuff you threw to the ground is poison,' Victoria said, 'and you will not see the flowers that lay hidden with that stuff. You will not see Pi or his father and you will not hear the sounds of the universe that play.'

'I didn't throw it down,' I said, 'I dropped it and I didn't mean to.'

'You did not drop it Alexander.' 'You threw it down,' Victoria said.

'I didn't throw it down,' I said again. 'I dropped it.'

Victoria paused and looked at me. 'Would you have dropped it two months ago?'

I looked at her.

I thought about it.

No, I would not have, I would have been careful. I would have tried it, I would have tried a lot of it and I would have stuck it in my pocket making damn sure it wasn't going to open being wrapped in paper as it was.

'I didn't throw it down,' I said again. 'I dropped it.'

'You don't even know what you do,' Victoria said. 'You don't know the interactions you are having. You are unaware of the interaction you are having with Pi. You are unaware of the interaction you are having with the presence that is filling your room and you are unaware of the interaction you had with that man and his cocaine.' Victoria pointed to the bird still perched on the branch. 'Interaction you just had with that bird and the interaction you just had with that flower.'

Victoria looked at me.

'As far as that man was concerned, you dropped his cocaine, but as far as Pi and his father were concerned you threw it to the ground.'

I looked at the ocean below and with our legs dangling over the cliff; I felt how very high we were. 'Well I can't argue with that,' I said smiling at Victoria 'but I didn't interact with that bird or that flower, I only looked at them. I only looked at them and thought what nice colours they have.'

'That is an interaction,' Victoria said, 'and where you take these interactions is up to you. How you let the interactions you have with the world around unfold, is limited only by you.'

'That stuff you threw to the pavement is poison. It stops the interactions you have. It stops any possible flow of real love between you and the world around you.'

'That stuff—it comforts the ego.'

'It comforts the ego and grounds you to it. It sends you powerfully, comfortably holding tightly to the constructs you believe yourself to be. It holds you tightly back. Blind within your own perception.'

'Never stop an interaction Alexander. Never stop an interaction you have with something, and see where it goes.'

'It goes forever,' Victoria said. 'It goes forever on a river of love.'

'Love is the only thing that does not stop. You cannot contain it.'

'You cannot control it and if you try you will step away from it and you will stop the interaction you are having and it will end with you holding to the perception you have.'

'If you limit the world to your perception, if you stop observing, you will stop seeing.' Victoria chuckled, as if this was as obvious as the ocean is salty.

'This love Alexander, it flows through other worlds, worlds of Pi and his father. Worlds of colour and worlds of sound. Worlds of spirit who are coming to you in your dreams.' Victoria clenched her hand into a fist and hit lightly to my thigh.

'These worlds of love Alexander.'

'Love is the only river flowing to them.' Victoria leaned towards me and whispered in my ear.

'People do not even know these worlds exist, but you can go there.'

'You can get there on a river of love.'

'A secret window, Alexander.'

Victoria's whisper was soft and her warm breath echoed through me.

'There is a secret window.'

I was tired, and after returning to the apartment I fell straight to the bed. My eyelids were heavy, and as I drifted from my apartment to the world of dreams I thought to rise early and paddle into the ocean. I thought of making my way to the mountains. I thought of Pi and his father and this presence Victoria said was speaking to me in my dreams.

I thought of this window she spoke of. A secret window. A secret window to other worlds.

Worlds that were crashing into mine.

Victoria lay next to me. She rolled over and faced me before I drifted off. She shuffled close. 'Listen to your dreams Alexander they are a part of you. Listen to them. Listen to yourself.' Victoria kept talking but I heard no more as my eyes fell comfortably shut.

Asleep to the world of dreams.

18. Truths come in dreams

I woke before dawn.

Victoria's arm was resting on my chest and I picked it up and placed it on the bed. I opened the balcony door a little letting a cool breeze enter the apartment, then filled the kettle and stood looking out to the ocean.

Dreams.

Such real dreams.

I looked through the open door to the bedroom. Victoria was asleep, and her arm was resting where I had left it. I closed the door and pressed the jug to boil.

Such real dreams.

I poured some tea and sat facing the ocean. I closed my eyes recapturing the dream that I had had, or rather the dream that I had been a part of.

I was riding a train.

The tracks it rode on could not be seen and all who entered and rode it could not be seen. I was the only one on the train, and as it bounced along the tracks, I sat looking out the window at the land it passed through.

I looked to see a large gathering of dark skin people.

None of them saw me or the train coming towards them. The train stopped and I got off.

As I walked into the thick of these people I turned around and around looking in every direction. Their skin was shiny and they were dressed in bright colours and they were dancing as if music had taken over their bodies. I walked through them, through their movement of colour, but I could not hear any music.

Their eyes were alive and they shone, glowing with happiness that moved around them. Such colours they wore were moving around me and the feeling of this group, the life that moved through them, the life that moved through their dancing, the feeling that moved through me as I stood in their dancing colours. It was wonderful. I stood surrounded by them, when I heard the music they were dancing to—or rather the music they were dancing with. It slid through the cracks of an invisible world. I stopped and I listened.

Music that only plays if you listen. Music that is always there. Music that is so strong and so full of life that if you stop dancing with it, you must have stopped listening. The music was coming from the earth.

They were dancing to the rhythm of the earth. They were giving their dancing to the earth and the earth was giving them a ground to dance on. They were dancing together. I never felt so alive. It ran through me. I heard it. I felt it. The rhythm of the earth. The sounds of the earth ran through them and through me, I turned around and around moving with these people and as I moved I felt them, decorated in their colourful clothes and dancing to the rhythm from the earth. Such incredible music. Such health ran through me, through every part of me. I laughed! I could not stop laughing.

It was so simple. Music, colours, dancing with the earth, the health that this brought. It flowed through them and it flowed through me. I closed my eyes and I raised my arms, laughing and dancing with them.

I was dancing with the earth!

I opened my eyes and I was back on the train. I looked out the window. The train was moving away from the crowd of dark skinned people.

'You must see something else,' a voice echoed through the train. I recognised her voice. I had heard it before. I looked around the carriage but there was no one. I looked back out the window and as fast as the train had brought me back aboard, it had stopped. I looked out the window. We were in the same place. The train had gone nowhere.

'Yes, this is the same place,' the voice echoed through the train.

'It is the same place, however, this is a different time.'

It was the same people. I stood looking at the same people, but they were not the same. They were no longer dancing. The life seemed to have been sucked out of them and the ground they were standing on was not the same. The ground was there, but it had no life. There was no music. They were no longer dancing with the earth. Life no longer flowed through them. There was no health. Their skin and eyes were discoloured, and the strength they once had could not be seen. The happiness they once had no longer flowed between them. Despair flowed between them. It was desperation and I stood in horror. How could this happen? They had been so alive. They had been so healthy and the air, the air had changed, sweeping through me, rushing through them like death.

Death.

All of them.

I felt it in the air. Death was coming for them all.

Death and sickness moved around them and their once colourful clothes that were now rags.

There was nothing that could be done. It was too late.

The weak fell to the ground and those who could stand waited until they could no longer.

I ran through them, panic running through me. I could not believe what I was seeing. A whole world of people plagued by starvation, disease and neglect.

I could do noting but stand in horror.

The train.

Again, I was back on the train and I did not want to ride it anymore, and I did not look out the windows until it stopped.

The train stopped in a city. It was a normal city and I got off and walked into a school. I entered a classroom where young children were painting and playing with blocks. Mess covered the floor, paint splashed the children's clothes and their smiles made me smile, filling me with happiness. Their happiness filled the room, and it filled me as I watched them laughing and playing.

Parents and teachers stood in the room, but they did not smile, they did not laugh, they just stood there with their arms folded talking awkwardly with each other.

Then I saw what the children were playing with. The coloured blocks they were building with had logos of food companies on them and the hangings on the walls were big credit cards with the names of banks inscribed on them. I turned to the teachers. 'Do you not see this?' I asked.

'Look at what is on your walls!

'Look at the blocks your children are playing with!'

'Look at what they are being taught!'

The teacher just stood with a confused look. She did not understand. I turned to the children's parents. 'Look! Don't you see?' But their expressions did not change. I pointed at the blocks, I pointed at the walls with credit cards hanging down them. 'Don't you see this?'

They did not see. They did not understand and they just stared at me, as if I were a madman. They stood dressed in their neat pressed clothes with their arms folded. They did not understand. The teachers and the parents were mechanical, there was no rhythm coming from them. The children looked up at me smiling, and their parents looked at me and tried to. They tried to smile, but they did not know how.

I was back to the train.

The train moved through the city and out of it. It moved through the countryside until it stopped by a large castle.

I stepped off the train and walked into the castle.

The carpet was soft and it smelt of roses. Huge silver and diamond encrusted mirrors hung on either side of the hall I walked through. I stopped as I came to a very large room and on his throne sat the King.

The King's face was strong, it was controlled and behind him stood an army of warriors.

The King stepped forward.

His frame was large, his shoulders as wide as my arms could stretch. He was larger than I thought a man could be.

'This is my castle,' the King said and he poked me hard with one finger and I almost lost balance and fell. 'This is my land,' the King said and he poked me hard again. 'My land,' he said, 'and I own everything on it.' The king jabbed me again and I toppled backwards and rolled to the floor. 'Including you,' the King said.

'Go to the city and make yourself useful,' the King said pointing to the doors from which I had entered, 'or join my army,' he said pointing at the warriors behind him. The King let out a deep laughter then turned facing his army.

'Fools who do what ever I tell them!' the King yelled.

The King threw is arms in the air, his face growing red with laughter. 'Fools!' he cried, 'I have an army of fools! He laughed harder. 'My kingdom and my people. They work for me and they fight for me!'

I looked at the King, his back to me, laughing at his own army. I looked at an armoured statue standing with a sword between its hands. I will take that sword and I will thrust it through the neck of the King. I stepped quietly towards the armoured statue. I took the sword from its grip and knelt, the Kings back to me ready to move and push the blade through his neck.

'Hey,' a woman's voice spoke softly. 'Hey,' she whispered.

I turned to see a woman standing by a corridor.

Her dress was thin and silky as was her long brown hair. Her eyes were a fiery green and although she looked as strong as the King, her voice was soft and gentle. I walked towards her.

She looked at the sword in my hand as she ran her fingers across my chest. 'Relax beautiful man,' she said, 'think of the treasure this land will bring you later. Come now and let us show you the softer side of our kingdom.' She pressed her lips close to my face, and I felt her warm breath and light perfume pass through me. She took my arm and we walked down a dimly lit passage of soft velvet walls, a passage that led to a large scented room. The scent of perfume moved through the air. Baths of hot water, oils and fragrance, fruit of every colour, women of every description. 'The King has much pleasure for you here,' the woman said, gesturing for me to enjoy the room of hot water, women and fruit.

I looked around the room. I looked at the silk fabric hanging down the walls.

'The stonewalls.'

I moved the silk hanging with the blade of the sword.

It was the same stone.

It was the same alive stone turning and moving as clockwork. A thousand clocks moving in the same place, turning and staring at me. An eye opened in the stone and it looked at me. It blinked and then disappeared back into the movement within the stone.

I am in the school!

I looked at the women who lay on soft cushions wearing silk and holding fruit.

It is not real.

I looked at the woman with her striking green eyes.

She is not real, I am in the school.

I looked at the stonewalls and they looked back.

The walls looked back and the women disappeared. The castle disappeared and before me looking at the stars, standing by the same spacecraft I had sat in before was the old man. The old man with the long white beard. He turned to me.

'You came back,' he said. He looked at the spacecraft beside him and he looked at me. 'You came back for this,' he said.

I looked at the spacecraft and I looked at him.

I stared at the old man. His baldhead. His long white beard, his large smile bearing a space between his front teeth. His penetrating eyes. 'What is your name?' I asked.

The old man did not move his gaze from mine. 'I do not go by names,' he said, 'and I might look different the next time we meet.' He peered closer toward me, 'and we might not meet here,' he said.

He looked again at the spacecraft and then into my eyes, raising a finger in the air. 'The school will always give you what you seek,' he said. 'It will give you the lessons necessary for you to find what you seek.' He looked back at the spacecraft.

'This spacecraft will take you right back to your lessons. Until you learn them,' he said. 'Until you finish the lessons you have come here to learn you will never fly the spacecraft.'

'It will fly you.'

19. Directions

I opened my eyes to see the early morning was moving forward. The dark sky was brightening and I heard the sounds of the shower, water pelting the tiled floor coming from the other room.

Victoria came out looking fresh. She looked at the ocean and then at me. Her eyes were awake, awake like she was looking through a telescope at distant planets. Awake like I had not seen eyes awake before. 'Shall we go?' she asked.

I pushed myself out of the lounge, 'yes,' I said.

Darkness had only just passed and we were the first to the beach. There were no boards in the water and there were no tents along the shore and we sat waiting.

The sun began to light more of the ocean and the first truck to arrive was my tattoo-covered friend with the boards I wanted. He stuck his head out of the window while coming to a stop, 'you are here early my friend,' he said.

He pulled up the truck, opened the back doors and pulled out long poles along with large pieces of canvas for his tent. 'You want the same board again?' he asked.

I looked at the surf. It was the same as yesterday, slow and gentle. 'Yes,' I said. He pulled out the two beautifully shaped longboards and threw a tub of wetsuits to the ground. I took a suit that fit better this time and we stepped into the ocean.

The first thing that hits you is the cold. You are in it and it quickly finds its way into your wetsuit to touch every piece of your skin. However, it does not take long for the small amount of water between your skin and the wetsuit to become warm from your body heat.

The second thing that hits you is the whitewash. The waves that have broken pushing to the shore. Here the waves are gentle and paddling through such whitewash requires little effort but when the surf is powerful it can push a person to their limits. It can show a person their limits and push them back to the shore. There are waves that no man can swim through.

We moved easily through this whitewash and paddled to where the waves were beginning to break. I slid off my board and swam down, down where it is colder and looked up at the board floating on the surface. The waves look different from down here. The waves feel different down here. The same body of water, a part of the same wave yet unnoticed from those who merely watch from the shoreline. What causes the wave to break is down here. I blew out and watched the air bubbles spiral, pushing for the surface, then swam up and slid back on my board.

Victoria sat looking toward the horizon at the sets were coming in. They were frequent and all that came were not quite overhead. She sat, waiting for something bigger unconcerned with the many good waves she was letting pass by. 'I want to go to Machu Picchu,' she said with her usual smile.

I looked to see a much bigger set was coming. Conversation is conversation but it stops when waves come. 'Good,' I said, 'I want to go there too,' as we both paddled hard towards this set.

Reading waves is something anyone can do. You know where you have to be. You have to be at the wave when it breaks. That's where the power is, when the wave coming in from the ocean meets shallow depths and rises up and crashes down on itself. That's where the power is and that's what pushes you along. Reading the wave, being in the right position at the right time to take the waves power and follow it along. Riding along the wave and following it as it breaks to the shore.

The set coming towards us was a nice size, it was somewhat overhead and as we paddled in the direction of the shore I felt its power push us easily along.

The boards that we had combined with the slow moving waves that were here made surfing casual and we both stood close to each other on the wave. 'I want to go to the Andes,' Victoria said.

I laughed. I guess you can have conversation while riding the surf.

'Today,' she said, 'I want to go today.'

We took this wave to the shore and began paddling out for another. I felt good. I always felt good in the surf but I was looking forward to the mountains and I was happy that Victoria wanted to come.

We stayed in the surf till late morning and arrived back at the hotel, as breakfast was finishing. We ate and showered, collected our laundry and headed to the bus terminal.

'Are you sure you want to take the bus?' I asked, as Victoria rummaged through her travel case. She looked up, 'yes,' she said, 'the bus will be good, we can see the land we pass through.' Victoria took a note and dropped her case on the table, and left to get some cool drinks.

I looked at her travelling case, there must be but one on the planet, green and Pink hyper colour and covered with small fairies. No wonder the cash was there, they probably thought it belonged to a small child and that there was nothing of value inside. Victoria put two drinks on the table and dropped a straw in each.

I drank from my glass and watched as a young man across the room threw his backpack on the floor, he wiped the sweat from his forehead and took a long drink from his water canister. He was screwing the lid on when something caught his attention. He stared at our table. He rested his drink bottle on the floor and walked over to us, his eyes fixed on Victoria's hyper coloured pink and green case. 'This!' he exclaimed.

He went to take it, but could not pull it from my grip and he let go while both Victoria and I stared at him. 'I found this,' he said, pointing at the green and pink case. 'I found this in the airport!'

I let the case fall on the table. Victoria's mouth opened and her eyes widened as surprise fused with curiosity swept her face.

'You did?' she said.

'Yes,' he said, 'on the floor in Lima airport. I gave it to lost property. Strange to see it here,' he said, a look of disbelief across his face. 'If I had known it was yours and you were going to be here I could have brought it with me,' he said as he laughed jokingly.

The man laughed at his own humour, but Victoria just stared at him. She stared as if he were a piece of a puzzle that had just been found. I stared at them both. I stared at the case on the table. If a pink elephant were to walk through the bus terminal, I would not be surprised. This world could not surprise me further. There was nothing more that could be more out of the ordinary.

However, I was wrong. What was ordinary was hiding under my nose. What was ordinary had been hiding from me my whole life. I was only beginning to smell it. Ordinary was only beginning to creep out from the shadows.

Luis was Chilean. He was travelling with a guitar, which playing on the street paid his expenses. If it did not, he carried a tent and a water bottle. He was also taking the bus to Cuzco, with plans of playing music and seeing the sights of the Andes.

'However, my reason for going now,' Luis explained, 'is to join a ten-day silent meditation not far from Cuzco.'

'Ten days silent?' I asked.

'Yes,' Luis said, smiling at my surprise that someone would be silent for ten days. 'It is time with yourself,' he said. 'Ten hours of meditation per day, for ten days,' he said.

I leaned back into my chair as Luis and Victoria spoke Spanish. I zoned out of the conversation and did not try to understand.

20. A new world

I didn't know man had built such buses.

We sat at the front on the second level of a two-story bus, enjoying a panoramic view through large windows. The seats were as comfortable as the leather sofas aboard the fishing boat and reclined into a bed. We were served hot drinks and meals and the three of us talked easily in-between watching the scenery and napping. The road wound through the mountains as we climbed the Andes and the panoramic seats we had let us enjoy the height and views of the mountain road.

Some twenty hours later we arrived and I woke up as the bus stopped. Luis collected his things from the overhead, 'Cuzco,' he said with a smile. 'A tourist hub and everyone travelling Peru will come here on their way to walk the famous Inca trail to Machu Picchu.' I looked out the window at the busy bus terminal. People from all countries stood dressed in trekking and colourful handcraft clothes.

'Three thousand metres above sea level, and some say,' Luis said, 'that Cuzco is the belly button of the planet. They say it is the birthplace of mankind.' I looked at Luis wondering how our planet could possibly have a belly button. The three of us piled into, and fitted snugly into, a small car being used as a taxi. Luis flicked through the pages of his guidebook and directed the driver to a place of accommodation.

We arrived at a budget guesthouse with shared rooms of bunk beds and communal showers and Luis checked into a room shared with thirty others. I stood in the lobby and my stomach began to tighten.

Loud music played from a bar situated in the middle of the accommodation and people were busy drinking heavily. I looked around the bar and my stomach tightened further. I wanted to go to the mountains. I wanted to walk to the highest mountain above the clouds. I wanted to look down and see nothing but mountains. The music from the bar combined with glasses being hit together filled my ears. I wanted to hear nothing. I wanted to be so high in the mountains that I could only hear wind blowing clouds around them.

I dropped my bag by reception and walked outside as Victoria talked with the girl behind the desk. I looked up at the sky, it was blue and the sun was still up. I looked at the mountains surrounding the valley the city was in. I looked at the higher mountains behind them, tall untouched peaks covered with ice.

Victoria came outside.

'Hey,' she said.

'I'm going to walk there,' I said, pointing to the top of the valley where the city ended and the taller mountains began. Victoria glanced inside at our bags that sat by reception. 'They have a private room if you like?' Victoria said.

We left our things in the room and the three of us walked towards the mountains surrounding the city. It did not take long before we arrived at the top of the valley where the thick of the city began to end, and we stood looking over the city. It was tight, if there was a space free it was being used, houses stacked on top of each other, pressed together with streets of tourist hagglers and produce sellers running between them.

The further we walked the less congested it became. We walked until there were no more buildings at all. Farmland and open space, nothing but that and us, until we approached a very large rock.

I breathed in the fresh air, it was quiet and I heard nothing but the sounds of our footsteps, nothing but that, until we walked closer to the rock. It looked as though this rock had been dropped from the sky, or perhaps it had risen from the earth.

Yellow tape strung around it forbidding some sections to be passed and inside the yellow tape was a group of men excavating, uncovering the stone under the earth and revealing the remains of what was once there.

It was the highest point in the nearby area and looking at the position of the sun

It would be our last destination this day. We walked to the top of this large rock and had a good view of the city, and the mountains in every direction.

To our left a group of young people stood listening to an old man. The old man's clothes were shabby and the group that listened to him were dressed in the latest hiking gear.

I looked down. To my right and below me, was a security guard sitting by what appeared to be an entrance into the rock sealed off by yellow tape and below him in an area also sealed off, the group of people were digging, slowly uncovering and reconstructing the remains of this site. Victoria paused, listening with interest as the guide spoke to his small group of tourists from Argentina.

'He says,' Victoria explained, 'this rock is a temple and that it used to be covered with gold.' Victoria smiled. 'He says, that many people have reported seeing flying saucers land here.' Victoria pointed to where he had just pointed, a flat clearing below us. Victoria listened as she translated the old man's words.

'Some people believe that this site along with others are connected to specific points of the earth, they believe that through sites such as this, people were able to, and some say still are, not only connect with the earth but pass through to the other worlds.'

Victoria spoke softly while listening, 'he says that sites such as this are connected to the stars.' 'He says, Victoria went on, 'that as the earth moves through the galaxy, the formation of planets and stars it is moving with, changes; they change according to the energy connecting them together.'

'He says, the formation of planets are following the formation of this energy and that this energy is throughout the universe. He says that this energy is a collective universal being that we are all a part of.'

'He says, that now our world is connecting with a new system of energy and a new system of stars and that our way of being will soon begin to change. He says, that the energy from other planets and stars will run through our planet and us. That it will soak through everything and we will begin to resonate not only with the earth, but also with the stars. There comes a new way for us to live on this earth. We will resonate with each other and all life of this world, and we will evolve to live in harmony with all.'

I watched as the old man talked with his hands, waving them in the air, as both us, and the group he was speaking to, listened.

'No more war,' he said. 'This will be in the past. This will be in the history books.'

'No more buying and selling. No more. No more ownership or attainment of wealth.'

'No more human ego. No more judgements towards others. No more fears.'

The man pointed away in the opposite direction and walked, guiding his group down the other side of the rock and out of sight. I was staring at Victoria. My eyes lit up. 'A temple, covered in gold?' I said. I glanced at the security guard in front of the entrance to the rock, then back to Victoria and Luis. 'Spaceships and travelling through the earth?' I said. I chuckled and pointed at the guard who sat looking bored, nursing his machete. 'That's a good enough reason for me to sneak in there,' I said.

Victoria smiled and a sparkle of fun shot through her eyes, but Luis did not share her smile.

I looked down at the guard and it was this moment that the universe spoke. It spoke to me and it said 'now is you chance.' Now is you chance to skip down the rock and past the guard, under the yellow tape and into the rock.

We stood looking down and the guard stood up. He waved he arms and yelled at a man who had crossed the yellow tape at the excavation below. The man appeared not to hear or see the guard and continued to walk further past the barrier he had crossed. The Guard was on his feet and moved quickly. Victoria and I looked at each other and we didn't need to say anything. We skipped down the rock to where the guard had been sitting, ducked under the yellow tape and in through the stone doorway.

I stopped immediately as I entered. The air was thick and heavy. This was not normal air. This was not a normal room. I stepped forward and the air felt heavier. I took another step and the air felt heavier still. I felt the air was becoming solid. As solid as I am. I stopped where I stood and looked at the stone. It was moving. It was the same stone from my dream, alive and moving as a thousand kaleidoscopes. I peered close at the stonewalls. Moving stone, like the inside of a detailed machine in operation. The movement changed as I looked at it. I looked at the wall and the movement of stone arranged itself and took the form of an 'eye' and then it opened, it looked at me, and then it blinked. I stared at the eye that was looking at me and then all around the room, eyes opened. In every piece of space of stone, eyes opened, and they looked at me. More eyes than I could count, eyes all around me looking at me. I stood staring in every direction.

I stepped further, air becoming heavier, taking the same form of the stone, bearing the same eyes, and becoming as thick as the rock. The air and the rock were the same and I was stepping into their mouth. The air was turning into the stone, looking with the same eyes, and the stone was becoming lighter, as light as the air. I stepped further. This room was swallowing me.

The air became indistinguishable from the stone. The stone became indistinguishable from the air and it took its grip on me. It was taking me. Eyes everywhere. As light as air, and heavy as stone. Both heavy and light, solid and transparent, this room, this fabric. I stepped into the stone. I stepped into the air. I stepped into this life-force and it stepped into me. The stone. The air. The eyes. The kaleidoscope fabric. It took me and I looked with ten thousand eyes.

I was the room.

I was the room and so was Victoria and I felt her, a part of the same body that filled this temple. I heard her and she was laughing, she was always laughing, behind every word and thought she had was laughter.

'This is a temple of dreams,' Victoria said. 'This temple will accommodate your thoughts. This temple listens and responds to your deepest thoughts, thoughts that you may not be aware you have. Here, like your dreams, your deeper thoughts will materialize and create your own world in this room, and it will be real. This temple will create any world here and any experience that will give you the teachings for what you wish to learn. You may create any world and take on any form and no matter how obscure or bizarre it may appear to be, it will be all that you know and as normal as the body you walk in now. Absorbed in what is most important to you, you will forget you are within the stone walls of this temple. And just like a dream you will not realise until you wake up.'

'If you hear your inner thoughts and have no dream to create, if there is no thought you wish to manifest, you will not create a world here and you will be free to continue, and enter through the walls of stone to a chamber that lies on the other side. A secret chamber, through a secret window. A secret window of yourself, guarded by your own thoughts.'

'There is no material door and only those who have let go of the material world may access it. Those who carry pain or hate, greed or desire will be subject to themselves and will manifest situations enough to live with a pure heart. Only those with a pure heart can pass themselves and the stonewalls.'

'A secret chamber on the other side.'

'A secret doorway to the beings that live within our earth,' Victoria laughed and I felt her smile in every corner of the room.

'A secret window to beings and life that is out of this world,' she said.

I looked around the room.

The air and the stone was air and stone. I felt my body as usual. The life-force had let go of me and I was back, standing on solid stone and breathing in normal air. I looked around the room, I looked at my hands and I looked at Victoria.

I turned to the wall with the chamber on the other side and placed my hands on it. I felt the room rush through me. It was fast. It was hard. It ran straight through me and took my mind. My mind took it. It gave my mind every food it could thirst for. My mind reached out to eat and the stone wall pushed me away. It pushed me hard and I fell back and rolled on the ground.

I stared at the stone wall. I stared at the distance it had thrown me.

Victoria stood looking down at me. She was laughing. 'I told you, didn't I?'

I looked up at her.

She looked down at me, 'welcome back to the three dimensional world,' she said. 'Perhaps this world is useful to you?' Victoria stopped laughing and just smiled.

'This world is our temple Alexander.'

I sat on the ground staring at the wall and flashed back to my dream with the old man.

I am the spacecraft.

This world is my school.

I am not driving my spacecraft.

The spacecraft is driving me. I am here to learn love, so I can fly myself.

I cannot hide from myself, and yes I thought, this world is useful to me. It is the greatest teacher that I could have.

21. New perceptions

We stepped from the inside of the stone temple to the outside, where I expected to be faced with a surprised security guard sitting next to his machete. We stepped out to see the guard in exactly the same position as when we had entered. He was waving his arms, shooing away the man who had crossed the boundary below. We walked back to the top of the rock where Luis still stood.

'That was quick,' Luis said.

I looked at him and I looked at Victoria.

'Yes,' I said, 'apparently it was.'

As we walked back to the city Luis and Victoria chatted away and I walked in silence.

The city was alive. European cafes and American bars were full and the streets were lined with shops selling handcraft, pottery and colourful clothes. We followed Luis who followed his guidebook, to the market where he said we would get a good meal for a good price.

I was not hungry. I could not think about food. I could only think about the secret chamber on the other side of the stone wall. I could only think, I was not driving my own spacecraft.

The market was busy and we sat amongst a hustle of shopping and groceries. I sat in my own silence, unconcerned with the items the market was selling. I sat listening as Luis spoke of the meditation he would be joining the following day.

'It's a beautiful place,' he said, 'surrounded by mountains and far from any town. There is a silence there,' he said. 'Time to go into your self.

'You rise before the sun does and begin meditation, ten hours of sitting each day.' Luis pushed his empty bowl to the side of the table. 'I love it,' he said, 'it is time to go deep. Time to let the grip that I hold on this world loosen, and see what's beyond my own grip.'

I leaned forward as Luis spoke.

I wanted to be surrounded by mountains. I wanted silence. I wanted the grips that I had on this world and the grip that it had on me to release. I wanted to fly my own spaceship. I wanted to drive myself to a new world and I wanted pain and poison to be nothing but a dream.

I drank from my glass of juice while listening to Luis. I wanted to join. I wanted to be silent. I wanted to be surrounded by mountains and sit solely with myself. I opened my phone and looked at the date, I was due back to the ship just a few days after this course would end. This is my world, I thought. It is my school and no one is going to make it different but me.

Victoria smiled, looking as though she might break into laughter as she let her drink sit on the table, then she lay down on the dirty market floor.

'What the hell are you doing?' Luis exclaimed.

I stared at her, as did the juice vendors and all those who passed by.

She looked at Luis and me, her huge smile shining as usual. I looked at her upside down face.

'Look at the tin roof,' Victoria said, 'look at the birds in the rafters.' She pointed at the roof. I looked up at the metal roof, that covered the large market, at the birds that sat in its rafters. I looked at Victoria's clean blond hair resting against the dark cement.

'You never know what the world looks like from here unless you are looking from here,' Victoria said, her eyes shooting in my direction.

'That floor is filthy,' Luis said with a look of concern.

'That is a part of being down here,' Victoria replied.

I smiled a half smile and Luis remained looking concerned. I smiled, not only for the dirt that was pressing against Victoria's clothes and hair, but for the attention she was drawing. I lay down next to her on the floor. I felt the dirty floor that had been stepped on by a thousand people rub into my hands. I looked at the rafters.

'You wont learn anything new if you don't experience anything new,' Victoria said. She spoke a little softer, 'see it's different down here.'

'Yes, it's different down here,' I chuckled.

And it was different.

We did not get confused looks from people passing when sitting at the table, and I did not feel the filth of the oily floor rubbing into my clothes, but I didn't care about clothes and I didn't care about the looks that anyone could give. I wanted new and I wanted to see the world differently and I was happy to sleep on the market floor for that. I lay there looking up at the tin roof and it hit me.

I had been walking through life seeing what I expected to see. I was walking through life living through my own perception, and now, down here perception was different. It was different and it was new.

I liked it.

The stone temple. It hit me!

The stone temple, the guide said it was connected to the earth. I thought about what Russ told me in the Amazon, energy running through him. Energy running through the earth.

I turned to Victoria, my cheek pressed to the cold floor.

'The earth,' I said, 'it's alive. It is alive and it is interacting with other planets, with the stars. The earth is a living being.'

Victoria laughed. 'Of course it's alive, did you just realise that now?'

'Yes,' I said.

22. Finally silence

The cold mornings of the Andes.

I pushed the covers away and dressed in the warmest clothes I had. I closed the door quietly, and again walked to the outskirts of the city. The sun was beginning to come up and as I reached the top of the valley it rose over the mountains warming me instantly.

I looked down over the city, feeling the warmth of the sun and the chill of the morning air. I sat and looked, watching the sun as it moved slowly into the sky. I sat with my hands in my lap feeling the heat and feeling the chill. I sat watching until the early morning was over.

With the rising of the sun came the rising of the people and I watched as the city woke up, like ants crawling out of their nest, people moved from their houses and into the streets and slowly the city became alive.

I brought fruit and bread and walked back. I passed people dressed in hiking clothes waiting by tour vans, in contrast to the few still drunk fuelled with cocaine, looking for the party that was over.

The three of us ate bread and fruit for breakfast, and then took a public mini van out of the city.

It was some hour's drive, to a small town where the meditation centre sat. The road followed the river, the river ran through the valley and the valley was surrounded with mountains, tall rocky mountains with icy tops.

The sun was higher in the sky when we arrived and there were no foreigners in hiking clothes here, yet, looking at the mountains there were plenty of places to go. The public mini-van left and it was the last vehicle that I would hear. It was quiet and still, still enough I could hear the grass creasing under my feet.

We stood and looked at the grounds surrounding the centre. Gardens of flowers and vegetables were beside every path, flowers and vegetables grew in every space there was enough earth for them. Fruit trees of pear and peach lined the perimeter and a field of corn stretched from the boundary of the property to the base of the mountains. The mountains shot up to the sky. I turned around while looking up. Tall rocky mountains in all directions and behind them were taller peaks above the clouds covered with ice and snow. I stood listening to the wind pushing through the mountains, pushing through the trees and down through the grass at my feet.

There was fruit and a selection of tea to choose from.

We filled in the forms with our personal information and I turned the page ticking no—no I did not have a mental illness—no I was not taking medication—and no I had no health problems.' Then I stopped. I re-read the next question.

Had I been using recreational drugs? What kind and how often? There were a few lines underneath left for an explanation. I needed more than a few lines. I looked at the question and paused. Perhaps they would not let me join? I rested the pen on the paper and thought for a moment. Then I picked it back up and I wrote.

I wrote small, so small it was barely legible. I wrote down everything and I wrote that I used when I had them, and that I always had them.

The fishing boat—it was my dry zone. The ship was my time away from heavy drinking, pills and junk. I hadn't had a drink since I had been here, and I had thrown the remaining junk to the river. I took a sip of my tea. I felt it move down and settle in my stomach. My stomach felt good. I felt good. I rested the pen on the paper. I had felt good since the Amazon. I had felt good since Pi had given me that medicine.

I was allocated a bed in a shared room and after putting my things where I was to sleep, we listened to a young woman explain, in both Spanish and English the course structure of the following days. The rules were based on enabling a person to focus solely on the meditation without distractions.

There were separate quarters for men and women, for both sleeping and eating. Females would sit on one side of the meditation hall and men would sit on the other and there was a code of silence, you were not to communicate with each other—not verbally, not with eye contact. You were not to distract others, such as wearing revealing clothing and so on. It was a vegetarian menu and during the stay you were not to kill anything. Not a cow, not an ant, not a mosquito.

She explained that if anyone felt like leaving to speak with one of the managers. She explained the benefits of staying and that they were there to support us in any way.

Those cooking were volunteers who took time away from their own meditation to wake people before dawn and prepare meals. There was a meditation teacher also volunteering her time, who was there to give guidance with the meditation. All based on donation. Those who attended in the past were supplying my food and what I would leave would go to those in the future.

That was that. Ten days of silence. Ten days of sitting.

I had spent countless ten-day periods drinking heavily, and countless ten-day periods killing fish.

Now I will sit.

23. Challenges met

They said not to communicate with others. They said not to make eye contact with others. They said to, try and sit still without changing your posture.

My cushion was thin. I was the last to enter the hall and it was the only cushion left by the door. I looked around the room. There were people with two cushions. There were people with three cushions. I looked at the man directly beside me. He sat on two cushions with one more propped under each knee. He had four. I looked at the people sitting on makeshift stools designed to make sitting for long periods comfortable. I placed my cushion on the floor.

It was 4:30am and the floor was hard and cold. The air was cold. I wore all the clothes I had and I was cold. I looked at the people with knitted scarfs and woollen hats. I looked at the warm blankets draped over their shoulders. I looked at the people with makeshift chairs and multiple cushions.

I closed my eyes and I did what they said. I did what the meditation teacher had told me to do. Pain ran through my knees and back, sitting in this terribly uncomfortable cross-legged position. Sitting on this terribly hard cold floor.

Two hours of this before breakfast. I looked at Victoria. She had a knitted hat and a thick woollen sweater. I wanted her hat and I wanted her sweater. Thirty minutes. I had been in this cold room for thirty minutes and I still had one and a half more hours before breakfast. I was to sit like this until late in the night. This for ten days.

I sat in that cold room. I sat feeling nothing but cold, nothing but pain as I uncrossed and recrossed my legs for temporary relief. This is as stupid as it gets. This hard floor. This cold room. A small bell sounded.

The ringing of a small bell meant the end of this sitting, and breakfast. I wanted to be the first to leave but as I went to stand my legs were so locked stiff I had to sit back down and massage some life into them. I watched as people left the hall, the open doors bringing sunlight inside. Sunlight and warmth. I looked at the ceiling and thought with some luck this room would heat up as the day moved on. I stood up to leave and looked where Victoria had been sitting. There was no cushion where she sat.

A large pot containing porridge sat on the table. Bowls that had contained seeds and nuts were next to it. I was the last to enter the breakfast hall and the large pot was almost empty, the bowls containing nuts and seeds to spice the porridge were empty. I scraped what remained to my bowl and sat down.

The porridge was bland, but it was so excellently hot, and I was happy to feel the morning warming slightly. I looked around the room at the mountain of food in some peoples bowls, covered in flavours from the table that was now empty. I looked at the jackets and knitwear that people were wearing. Two hours, I had been here for two hours. I poured a hot tea, and sat, until that awful bell rang again.

The day became warmer, but it was still cold. The same pain ran through my knees and back as I sat on the same hard floor. The same discomfort. The same sitting. Just sitting.

Observe the pain they had said, observe it as a sensation and observe it pass away. Observe it as nothing more than a sensation. However, the pain did not pass away. The floor did not become softer and although warmer, it was still cold. My only comforting thought was to leave. To go back to what I should be doing, back to the ship where I had a soft sofa in my cabin, a heater, and whatever I felt like for breakfast.

I sat feeling the pain. I sat feeling the cold and every time the bell rang I was relieved. There was no dinner, no food after midday and I went to bed hungry.

The following days were the same, nothing had changed. Nothing except I brought a blanket to the meditation hall. A cheap itchy blanket, however it was warm.

I didn't care about the others, I didn't care they took more food than was to go around, and I didn't care that the man next to me had four cushions when Victoria had none. I wanted to leave and I wanted to leave now.

I thought there was something here for me. I thought, after meeting Victoria, and this man Luis finding her case, that I should be here. I wanted a new path. I thought this was my path. I thought this is where I should be. I didn't care if other people wished to stay. I did not. There was nothing for me here.

I went to bed that night with my bag packed by its foot, and the following morning I did not wake up to the volunteer ringing that bell at four am. This morning I did not hear the bell and I continued to sleep, dreaming as I slept. It was this dream that made me stay, for if I had awoken with that bell, I would have taken my bag and walked out the gate.

I had dreamt such a dream before; that I was something other than myself, a school of fish and I saw through many eyes. However, this night I was not a group of fish. I was of all things, a chameleon. I was dreaming that I was a chameleon. I was a chameleon and I was in the jungle.

Different plants of all colours surrounded me, green leaves, red leaves and flowers of bright colours filled the jungle and I was standing in the thick of it. Dark purple veins ran through the leaves that sprouted from the branch I held to and the leaves and flowers stretched in every direction.

I felt the body I was in and I looked through its eyes—my eyes—very different eyes. I could see through the eyes of the chameleon and I could see clearly. The colours, the different shades of colours, the different textures and detail of all the life around me, and depth of intricacy of the branch I stood on was something I saw in a way I never thought possible.

Not only was it my surroundings I could see. Not only was I looking through the eyes of the chameleon. I was looking through the eyes of the branch and I was looking through the eyes of the plants that surrounded me. I was looking at the plants from the chameleon and I was looking at the chameleon from the plants.

I could see the branch I stood on from every part of it. Inside the branch and outside the branch, every fibre within the branch, my eyes were in the space between the smallest fibres that made up the branch, the plants and the chameleon. I was seeing through the eyes of everything, I was seeing through the eyes of the space-in-between-everything—and there is a lot of space—and my eyes were everywhere. A yellow flower sat next to my tail, growing from the branch I held to. The branch, a smooth silky texture on the outside, yet moist and wet through the inside.

I saw with very fine detail the inside, an inside that connects us all. The inside that runs through everything. Through the veins of the plants, through the strong hard timber rooted deep in the earth. I flowed through them and into the earth. Connected. The branch that I stood on is connected to the other plants and all of them are connected to the jungle, and the jungle is connected to the earth.

Consciousness flows through the plants. I felt them. They are alive. The same consciousness that I perceive the world through is the same that they do. Only they look through a much different system of life, nothing like my own. Connected to the earth. Connected to each other. Connected to the jungle. I stood on the branch looking through the eyes of the chameleon, in direct contact with the earth and all the life around me. Alive, the jungle, consciously alive.

I changed the colour of my tail to match the colours of the yellow flower.

My soft bumpy skin, changing from the inside.

I felt the flower. It shared with me the being it is and the world it is connected to. I was a part of it. I could see through it, the plant that it grew from and the jungle it is connected to. I could change the colour of my skin simply by resonating with my surrounding. I was connecting with them and they were welcoming me. I could shift into their world on the inside and watch my colours change on the outside. My tail changed to match the yellow of the flower. I began to camouflage to the branch I held to and the jungle around me. Invisible to all without the eyes of a chameleon.

Camouflage.

I sat up in my bed, awoken by the presence in my room. It was Victoria. The room was empty apart from her standing in it. She saw me, and relief swept her face, 'I thought you had left,' she said. 'I didn't see you in the meditation hall,' and with that she walked out the room.

I lay back down only to wake again by the gentle shake of a young volunteer. He spoke softly, releasing his hand from my shoulder when I opened my eyes. 'Try to meditate,' he said. I sat up, realizing I had overslept. I got out of bed and felt the icy morning. As I dressed, that little bell rang for breakfast.

Two hours—I had slept and missed the first two hours of the day's meditation. I looked at my packed bag on the floor. I sat on the side of my bed looking at it until the bell stopped ringing.

I decided to stay.

I blew out a long breath and walked toward the breakfast hall. I stopped half way and thought of Victoria. She had been in my room. Why had she entered my room? Why was she not in the hall with the others? I thought of the dream I had and wondered if that was the world the chameleon knew.

24. A different reality

Today I was the first to enter the breakfast hall and the large pot of porridge was full. I took a small helping along with a banana and walked outside. The sun was hiding behind the clouds and as usual, the morning was cold. I sat looking at the meditation hall.

I thought about the North Sea.

I had been cold before.

I thought about the smell of the ship and fish blood splashing my face.

I threw the banana skin to the garden.

Perhaps it was better here.

I did not wait for the bell to ring before going into the meditation hall, and when I entered I was the only one there. Some comforts lay by other's sitting positions. I looked at mine.

I took my cushion and placed it where Victoria sat.

The hard floor was even worse and the pain ran through me as soon as I sat down, the same familiar pain. The same familiar pain I had felt for the past three days ran through my knees and back. I threw the blanket over my head and let it drape to the floor, it helped but I was still cold.

Cold and pain. That is why I'm here. I will stay here, I will sit here for seven more days feeling the cold and feeling the pain. I closed my eyes and felt the cold. I felt the pain. Observe the pain they had said, observe it and watch it pass away. Nothing is permanent they said. Observe the sensations you feel and watch them pass away.

I drifted off thinking about my dream as the chameleon, looking through its eyes, looking through the eyes of the plants and the jungle.

It clicked.

The penny dropped and it hit the floor, echoing loudly through the hall. The dream as a chameleon. The stone temple above the city. It clicked.

I am not my pain.

I am viewing the world through the being that I am. I am feeling through it. However, I am not it.

I am, what I am holding onto. It clicked. I am feeling the pain I am holding.

This world is my school. I am creating my own surroundings here and living through what I am holding onto.

I could hold onto any pain.

I could hold onto anything.

The stone wall had thrown me away, not allowing me to enter. It had thrown me back to where I was, back to the world I was holding. I needed to let go of myself to enter the stone wall and I need to let go of the pain I am holding in order not to feel it.

I am viewing myself through the things I am holding. I am holding onto myself, to that which I believe to be fundamentally concrete.

I let the blanket covering me fall to the floor and cold air that was hitting the blanket hit me. I felt the pain, running through my knees and spine. Pain that is not mine. It does not belong to me.

I watched the physical pain. I watched it move and I watched it change. The meditation teacher was right. It is not permanent. I watched the pain move around my legs and back. I did not accept it. I watched it. I felt myself. I felt myself and I felt something new. I felt new physical sensations running through and around my body. Smaller sensations hiding, masked by the pain. Tingling over and through my skin and with the new physical sensations hiding under the pain were new feelings that came with them.

This is my school and I am bound by what I am holding. What I hold onto subconsciously is manifested physically and underneath, as I let go of both the mental and physical me, was a completely new me that I had never experienced before.

I sat; glad that I had stayed and I understood why people practiced this. I understood why they had not spoken of such wonders in this practice. I understood why they simply said, sit and practice. I had to experience myself for myself and I would not have believed the world they were entering.

A tingle.

A tingle running over the surface of my skin. All over my skin. Every part of my body, a vibration. Underneath the pains and ideas that I held myself to, was a world I was connected with. A world I could not feel or see when holding so tightly to another. A vibration. A vibration running over my skin, through my skin, through my body and through the air, a vibration that passed through all things.

I sat perfectly upright.

I was the vibration that filled this room and I understood why people sat. I understood why people sat in meditation and I understood why they sat with their back straight. Sitting in this vibration I could not sit in any other way, for running through me was a beam of light and I was sitting aligned with it.

 I was sitting aligned with a part of myself.

I let go of that which bound me to my physical body and I looked through a much different body. A much lighter body. A body of much lighter matter. Matter so light it is not even apparent on the physical plane. Yet matter it is - and a body I was still in. Still very much me.

I stood, looking down at myself. There I sat with my eyes closed and my legs crossed, light passing through my body and out the top of my head, continuing on for as far as I could see.

I rose into the air.

I left the ground and looked down on the people sitting silently in the hall. I drifted back to the floor and looked at myself, I looked at myself and at the light that ran through me.

'That light is you too you know.'

I turned, it was Victoria.

She smiled, 'Thanks for the cushion,' she said. 'I'm glad you stayed.'

She waved her hand and passed it through my body. I watched her hand pass in and through me, and out of the other side. I felt her, I felt her thoughts run through the air, through this vibrational soup we were in.

I looked at myself. My eyes were closed, my legs were crossed and my hands were resting in my lap. I looked at the light running through my body—or rather it seemed my body was coming out of the light.

I moved closer to myself, looking at the light surrounding and moving through my body. It was just as Russ said. Light passed through every living cell in my body. Every form of life in my body had the same light that ran through me, run through them.

Every separate life form inside me had this light running through them and they all appeared to come out of this light. They were connected together through a pattern. A vastly intricate, geometric formation of light that connected each moving cell to each moving cell. The cells in my body were following and moving to the geometry that the light was forming. The geometric formation was moving; it was changing and the interactions within me changed with them.

A kaleidoscope.

A kaleidoscope of constant changing formation, from one pattern to another. Moving geometry of light within myself. Victoria leaned closer toward me. She pointed at the light spiralling out the top of my head, stretching as far as I could see.

'You are connected too,' she said, 'to all that you interact with of this world, you are a part of a vast geometric formation, like that which is inside you. As is the light spiralling through you, connected to the stars and the earth. As are the planets and the stars connected, forming the same geometry that is within you, the same geometry that you form with others. Consciousness runs through each planet and consciousness runs through each star.'

Victoria looked from the changing movement of light connecting the particles inside me to the light stretching up through myself towards the stars. She was smiling. 'Shall we follow it?' she said.

I looked at the light running through me and I looked up.

Victoria rose into the air and passed through the roof of the meditation hall.

I rose into the air looking down on the silent people sitting in the hall then moved through the roof to the outside. Victoria was standing with her arms stretched out on the edge of the roof. I had never seen a smile as alive as hers.

I looked around. The vibration of this world is more exhilarating than any fresh breeze could be. Victoria stepped off the roof and drifted gently over the garden, over the fruit trees. Never had I felt so exhilarated, not in all my life. There was nothing I could compare this to. I stepped off the roof and I flew. I flew over the garden. I flew over the grounds of the meditation centre and I looked up at the mountains surrounding the valley.

I rose higher into the air until I could see the long river running through the valley. I could see more as I rose higher and higher. The grounds of the meditation centre became smaller and smaller until I was level with the tallest mountain.

I could see over the land, to Cuzco, mountains in every direction. I looked to see Victoria sitting on the top of the tallest nearby peak.

She sat comfortably looking over the land. She looked calm and at home in a world she seemed familiar with. I rose up to where she sat and joined her on the rock looking over the valley. Victoria pointed to the earth below, 'do you see them?' she asked.

I looked down at the Earth. I looked at the light that surrounded and connected our world. I looked up to see that this light was connecting the stars. Surrounding our planet, connecting us with other worlds. A pattern in the sky. The same vastly intricate pattern of light I has seen in myself, also connected the stars.

'Do you see what's wrong?' Victoria asked.

I looked at her.

'No,' I said.

'Humans have lost connection with their own light.'

'They have lost connection with the earth, themselves and others, and the energy passing through them is hardly moving through the connections that join us together. They are living separate from the earth, from each other and they are becoming sick because of it. They are becoming sick in every way a human can become sick.'

'They are suffering internally and externally through lack of sharing. They suffer mentally, physically and economically.'

'They must. We must. Learn to share,' Victoria said. 'Share, not only the material world, but also the light that is running through us. It is our sustenance. It is us.'

'We must share love.'

'The earth and the stars are always moving Alexander, they are always growing.' Victoria looked hard at me.

'A long time ago our ancestors were here and the earth moved into a new formation, a great formation, connecting with many other worlds. Those who lived through the connections that bind us together moved into our collective self and into this new formation and they moved to new worlds that they were resonating with.'

'But not all were in tune, not all were connected to each other, not all shared love. Not all shared themselves with the earth, and there were those that remained.'

'Those who remained were separate from each other, those who lived holding tightly to their material wealth. They did not know or feel the connection with others or the earth. They did not know the light that they were, and they did not know that they stopped the energy flowing through them to others. They did not let the light of others pass to themselves. They did not live through love and their inner structure did not match that of the formation that the planet was joining. Their inner sound played to another frequency. They stayed and continued to sleep in the physical world.'

I looked at the light that passed through our world, and got the feeling it moved in many different directions. That it formed every possible formation, and that I could be a part of whatever I chose.

'Ancestors?' I asked.

'Yes, our ancestors.' Victoria smiled. 'Would you like to meet them?'

I looked at this girl, her legs dangling over the peak of the highest rock in the valley.

'Yes,' I said. 'I would like to meet them.'

Victoria's smile increased and I felt the energy rise inside her.

'I love going there,' she said

She stood up and looked down at me.

'We will need a vehicle,' she said.

25. Meeting the ancient wise ones

Balancing on the peak behind me was a hyper coloured pink and green convertible.

'Where did that come from?' I asked.

'Come on, get in,' Victoria said as she climbed into the drivers side. The wheels folded underneath its body and the car rose up, letting out a deep low humming noise.

Victoria's smile was huge. 'Come on get in!' she said.

The sounds of the car, the same sounds that had ran through the spacecraft in my dream. It was many sounds. It was high tones. It was low tones. These vibrational tones, all of them one sound. It was a symphony of notes.

I climber into the passenger seat, and Victoria turned to me as she pushed a button in the centre of the dashboard. The dashboard folded in on itself, revealing a screen, a display of swirling galaxies. Victoria pointed to the navigation system. 'You can go anywhere you wish,' she said. She zoomed in randomly to a swirling galaxy and coming into view on the screen was one of the many planets there. 'Look how they live,' Victoria said.

I looked at the screen. It was one mess of movement, like fish swimming in the ocean, yet I could not distinguish between the ocean and the fish. Movement of colours and activity, colours moving and blending with other colours, making new colours. I gave Victoria a quirky look. 'Shall we go there?' I asked. 'No,' Victoria said, 'this is just one of many worlds.'

Victoria zoomed in to another planet and pointed to it. 'We are going here,' she said.

I looked at the screen to see a thin rather tall and very humanlike being. He was walking through a forest of some description and he seemed to be extraordinarily happy. He looked as though he was having an extremely good day. What ever it was that happened to this being, he could not be happier.

I watched him and I felt as though I felt him. I leaned closer. I could feel him. Through the dashboard of Victoria's car I could feel this being and I could hear him. I felt him and I felt the world he was walking through. I understood why he was so happy. He was viewing the world in an astonishing way. It reminded me of the chameleon.

He was interacting with all life around him. He was connected with all life around him. I felt him and I watched him. He was singing, and he was not walking through the jungle, he was dancing. He was singing and dancing as he made his way through the jungle—and the jungle was singing with him. They were singing and dancing together. I stared at the screen.

I have been to this world,' Victoria said. 'I was there when I was a young girl and they told me of the instrument that is the human being. They spoke to me of separation from one's own self and they spoke of the love that flows through the fabric of all things. Their world taught me there is nothing to fear.'

Victoria looked at me, her hand gripped around the handbrake, her thumb positioned ready to release it. 'Are you ready?' she asked.

'Yes,' I said.

Victoria released the handbrake and as she did the car truly came to life. The humming noise became higher and both lower pitch at the same time. The humming so low, so high that it vibrated the car into a different plane. A different vibrational plane where such sounds came from. An ancient power pushing through every piece of the car's body. The seats became more comfortable, fitting snugly around me. Powerful humming drove us up, rising higher over the cloud line, over the Andes. We kept going up.

I looked down at the continent of the Americas. Huge rivers ran through them, like the veins within a leaf. You forget they are connected to the ocean until you are up here. Mountains that run through many countries, running through the many borders, mountains that were there long before borders were. I looked at the changes in landscape from the equator to the poles, and from the coast to the coast. We continued to rise higher and looking down, I could see the rotation of the earth, the shadow upon it, where the sunlight would soon fall, bringing morning to some and night to others.

Victoria stopped the car and we stayed looking down for a moment. The earth. Stars littering the sky in all directions. It was a sight—the stars—stretching forever as far as could be seen, stars behind stars behind stars, galaxy after galaxy. Big spiralling galaxies.

We sat in the car looking at the black space littered with sparkling worlds. I sat looking at our world. A world I had never seen from here before. We sat for a time until Victoria touched the planet we were heading to on the screen. She turned to me. 'Now we go,' she said.

Sucked through the dashboard of the car! My eye fixed on the planet we were headed for. Fast. Faster than time. So fast that time seemed to be nowhere. Too fast to check if there was any car at all, and as fast as I had been thrown through the dashboard toward this foreign galaxy, I was thrown back, comfortably to the passenger seat of the car and we were orbiting the planet that was our destination.

I stared at how enormous it was, thousands of times the size of Earth and it was green and there was water.

In front of the dashboard where the display of galaxies had been, was now an old cassette player. I turned the dial trying to tune the radio. 'There is no radio here,' Victoria said. 'Look' and she pointed around us, 'there are no satellites either.'

'This world is old,' Victoria said. 'It is much older than earth and the physical world we left does not exist here. No being here dwells in such dense matter. They are still a part of heavy matter, but they do not spend their time perceiving through it. Like the trees,' Victoria said. 'The spirits of the trees do not spend their days blowing in the wind for thousands of years as their physical body does. 'Certainly not,' Victoria said, 'they are much busier than that.' Victoria looked at me. 'If you came here on a rocket ship with your radio to earth and food rations, you would find no one. You would radio to earth that there is nothing here but a wasteland. You would say is looks uninhabitable and take some samples.'

We moved closer towards the planet and Victoria pointed to the surface. 'Look at their buildings,' she said, 'see their shape and look where they are placed.' We moved closer still to what looked like a city, or a type of city.

Their buildings were spread out. They were not congested like ours on earth.

'They are a direct link to other stars and to other galaxies,' Victoria said. 'The shape of their buildings and the formation they are in is not just a symbolic replica of the geometry within their world. It is a way for them to connect with their inner structure, and to connect with the stars—their outer structure. They watch themselves as they watch the stars and they walk in balance with their world.'

'This is a harmonious world,' Victoria said, 'and there is no buying or selling here. There is no ownership of their surroundings and you will see why when we arrive.'

We flew down closer and it appeared Victoria was going to land in a large clearing of neatly cut stone especially designed for visitors. As we approached I saw how absolutely huge the trees were. A thousand times the height of anything I had seen on earth, stretching over the land as far as I could see. 'They must be hundreds of thousands of years old.' I looked up at how truly huge they were, as high as mountains.

'They are much older than that,' Victoria said, as we landed softly in the large clearing. I sat in the car looking up at the trees. Never did I think trees could be so incredibly huge. I looked around. The grounds were clean, they were neat and it didn't look as if someone kept them tidy. It seemed that the grounds kept themselves in the order they wished to be. Tiny flowers poked through the grass by the tree's trunks and standing some distance away at the entrance to a interestingly spiral shaped building was three incredibly human like, yet unmistakably alien beings. There was no question that they were here to meet us, as they stood and waited.

Victoria and I stepped from the car and as soon as I placed one foot on the ground I understood. These people did not own or sell anything. As soon as I touched the ground I understood. You could not own this!

She said the trees were more than just standing pieces of wood. I understood. The trees, the spirits of the trees, the beings that they were hit me like a speeding train—and I was in their tunnel.

I touched the ground with but one foot and they were there. Old as time. They were there and this was their world.

I had entered their world and they were there. They came to me and they were looking. They came into me, curious of the visitor that had arrived. The trees of this world—they were not what I would have expected. They moved into me, They moved through me—through all parts of myself—through parts of myself I did not know were there, but I felt them. I felt them and I felt what they were.

It was not like meeting a person. It was not like encountering an animal. It was an encounter with a life force of substantially greater evolution than myself. A highly evolved life form of complex intelligence. Complex to me, for I did not understand the world in which it lives. I was only beginning to see the world that I had lived in my whole life, a world that I knew little about. The trees, they knew, and they knew I did not understand. They knew what stage of growth and evolution I was at. They knew and they moved deeper inside.

I stopped where I stood as the spirits of these trees moved. Strong and old, stronger than anything I had felt before. Their strength filled me, their strength, standing so tall, so still for so long, strong as they are tall. Old and wise. They came to me. They moved slowly and they moved gently, the spirits of these trees moved, searching the being that was new to their world.

As many they entered. As one they entered. They were many yet connected and moved through me as one.

They held great intelligence. Information. Searching, scanning, curiously seeking every piece of myself. Reaching to the sky, as tall as mountains, I stared at what is their physical body, as they began to stitch and weave themselves into me.

Victoria stood as motionless as I did, captured by the spirits of this world and then I shook. They shook me. They shook me loose. They shook me loose from myself. Their vibration. They were vibrating inside me and my structure was shaken apart. No longer were there particles of myself holding myself together. I was shaken apart. They shook me into the smallest pieces that held me together and they were examining me. Every part, every little part, there was nothing of me they did not see. They poured into me. They poured in and they filled me, connecting themselves with me. Connecting me with a vibration. They vibrated around every particle of the body in which I was travelling. They vibrated through parts of myself I didn't know I was. They vibrated until I was vibrating to the same frequency as they were. They were bringing me to the same movement as their world. They were binding me with themselves. They were binding me with the same light that passed through them. They were binding me to the formation of their world.

I stood. I could not walk, gripped by the spirits of this world and I watched as the three alien beings walked towards Victoria and I. The three of them stopped before us, but it was not them who spoke. It was the trees.

Thank you was what they said.

Towering, as high as the tallest mountains of our earth, their trunks as wide as our tallest buildings.

'Why?' I asked.

'Thank you for accepting us,' they replied. 'You are welcome here,' they said.

I felt different. I felt sharp and I felt clean.

Sharpness. Incredible sharpness and immense clarity. I looked at the trees. They had shared themselves with me. They had taken me to the vibrational plane in which they live. They had not given me their knowledge, yet they had shown me their clarity, that I may attain such knowledge for myself. I felt strong, stronger than I had ever felt before, strong and fearless. I looked at these trees. They are strong and fearless. They do not live with a pinch of fear.

I looked at the alien beings standing before Victoria and I. They were all different heights. Their bodies were slim and looked elastic. Their fingers were long and slender, and their huge eyes the size of my palm took up most of their large heads. I stared at them and they stared at me.

The smallest of the three was shorter than me. He was shorter than Victoria. He stepped forward.

There was a language here.

There was language in the wind. There was a language in the trees, a code of information that passed through the life of this world. I felt it, the life in the trees, the life in the earth. It did not speak in words but it was there. I did not listen in words but I could hear. An ancient language long forgotten, a language I understood. A language we all understood. A language that passed through all life, a language that is a part of us. A language we haven't listened to in a long time. A language of the universe that all things could speak through.

This being, his huge eyes. His light green skin.

He stood effortlessly.

'You hear what you are able to receive,' the being said, gesturing toward the towering trees and the two other beings who stood on either side of him. Both were taller than him; both looked different yet the same, with the same large head and the same huge eyes, yet easily distinguishable with subtle differences. The same thin elastic bodies with light green skin.

This alien being seemed to look directly at both Victoria and me at the same time. 'We are children of this world,' he said. 'We are the youngest that live here.' He looked up at the trees. 'They have been here longer than we have,' he said. 'They were here long before we ever came to this world and just like on your world they support us here,' he said. 'Their spirits are awake in many planes of existence.' The small alien being took a step forward.

'They support you through your physical embodiment. They are supporting you during this process as you travel the earthly planes. Timber, oxygen, medicine and food. They support you, and not only in the dense material world, but here in the lighter material worlds. Here they are giving you a different food, and a different air to breathe.'

The eyes of this small being seemed to dance as he spoke. I stared into them.

Everything.

He was showing every part of who he was, he was holding onto nothing. He was letting every part of everything that he was pass into me. He turned his head slightly more in my direction and I felt even more comfortable as he did. I felt even more at home and relaxed, sharp, clear and relaxed.

'We are all the same energy,' the small alien being said, 'the one being'. It is us. We are it. Together we share the same body, and we share it with each other. He stepped further forward. He spoke again and his words seemed to adjust to my own thoughts. 'We can form the energy of ourselves to become anything we wish,' he said.

His words grabbed me in a way I had not been grabbed before and I took a step closer.

I stared at him. I stared at the three of them. They were changing. They were moving. They were thin green alien beings yet they were shifting. They were not only thin alien beings. They were more. They were much more, and I could see them.

In the same place at the same time, every part of them. As if they had lived the life of every creature to ever walk my earth, I saw all of them. Every insect. Every animal and countless people. As if they had lived the lives of countless other forms from countless other worlds too, they were all there. I could see them all. Creatures I had never seen before, entities that were incomprehensible. They were all there in the same place. They were living through all of them. They were all of them at the same time and all of them were looking at me.

Multi-faceted movement of form; countless beings sharing the same space. They were countless faces, they were countless forms and I felt inside myself the many as they were many, yet I did not know how to show it. I did not know how to interact with them in this way. They were more than a million. It was countless. I became lost. I could not focus. It was too much. I did not know how to stand before them.

The trees roots seemed to take hold of me.

Their branches moved inside me, blowing gently with the wind that was about to push me down. They had not left and they felt me. They understood how I felt and they held me, they held me strong, as strong as they are. They did something. They were everywhere, and they built a bridge between us. They allowed me to see them as only the thin green beings. The trees held my eyes to see a form that was suitable for me.

They were laughing.

The trees were laughing and the alien beings standing before me were laughing. Thin green alien beings, laughing with the trees, laughter that filled me, filling me in a wonderful way. Laughter that was sitting on a solid ground of happiness. These beings, they had happiness so solidly ingrained on such a firm foundation that they were happiness. I felt the love that is what they are a part of and it was laughter that followed. I felt that they were not only laughing, but that they were their laughter. I felt that they were not only showing me love, but they were this love. They turned and walked towards the spiral shaped building and Victoria and I followed.

26. The future task

Underneath the towering trees, we walked behind the three alien beings towards the very tall, spiral shaped building.

Its huge strong base was fixed firmly to the ground and what could be used as steps were the different levels of stone as it spiralled upward. I looked at the huge round base and I looked up. In the distance I could see the tip of this building, a thin point of stone. I could not see where the stone had been joined. It looked as if the entire building was carved from the same rock.

We stood by the entrance and the smallest of the three turned to us. There was so much inside of him smiling. Every being that he had ever lived as was smiling, and this smile pushed through to the green being's face, giving him a warm smile that was almost cheeky. He pointed at the building. 'The rock is the house of the crystal pools,' the being said.

'Liquid crystal runs through our world, as do the arteries and veins that run through flesh and plant matter. Liquid crystals flow through our world. This material flows through the galaxy and as our star moves through the universe, it is the beings of crystal that are the bridge between worlds.'

I felt he had more to say and I got the distinct impression Victoria was hearing something very different to me. I felt the trees. I felt the their roots growing deeper. The trees were translating, sifting through the alien's many appearances and allowing me to see what was suitable, sifting through his words, through the vast amounts of information he was sending and I was hearing but a segment of what he was sharing. I was hearing what I was able to hear. I was hearing what was relevant to me. I looked at Victoria and wondered what kind of dialogue she was receiving.

'You will meet yourself in these walls,' the being said.

'You are the spirit of the stone that flows through this planet. It is the same spirit that flows through your planet, and within the depths of yourself you are a part of this being. Within these walls you will meet the parts of yourself that are residing within them. Time does not exist there, as it does not exist when the confines of physical matter have been stripped away. You will exit when you find what you seek.'

The three of them entered the spiral building and we followed, and I looked up. There was no roof. From the outside it was clear that this building reached into a point and its spiral formation was apparent, but from the inside it was different. There was no roof to this building, and swirling above me were huge clusters of stars. A galaxy swirling in motion, an array of colours hazing over spiralling stars and a beam of light stretched from a pool beneath my feet to the stars high above.

I looked into the pool. It looked solid. I could see my reflection perfectly and that of the galaxy shining down from above. I reached down and dipped my finger to feel this liquid pool. It was solid. I was touching a solid material, yet the pool, it rippled. It rippled with the touch of my finger. I watched the circles ripple to the edges of the pool and again back to the centre, gently bumping into each other. It looked like liquid. I touched it again. It was as hard as glass, and it stretched down as far as I could see.

I looked around the room. Victoria and the alien beings were gone.

A woman's voice echoed softly around me. Her voice came from every direction, from the stars above and from the pool below. I recognised her voice. It was soft and gentle. It was the same voice that spoke in my dreams. The voice that had whispered, that 'what I need is a little wind.'

I looked around the room and then up to the spiralling galaxy. I looked back to the pool by my feet, which had ceased to ripple and was once again still.

Echoing through the stone walls. Powerfully filling the room and for a moment her words was all that there was.

'Reflection,' she said. 'What you need is a little reflection'

I looked into the crystal pool. I looked at my reflection staring back at me. My reflection, the ordinary reflection of me. I stared into the pool at myself staring back, and then, my reflection, it began to age. My reflection aged right before my eyes, but I was not getting older. I was getting younger. I fell to my knees with my hands pressed against the pool's solid surface, watching as my life began to unfold. I saw myself in the liquid pool, but it was not through my perception that I watched the events of my life. It was through the eyes of the spirit whose body was this liquid. Through the eyes of this solid crystalline pool, through this soft woman's voice, I saw through her eyes and her eyes were everywhere.

She was a part of me, and a part of everything else, and I was watching myself through the eyes of everything. I stared, reliving the events of my life as they unwound before me. I watched every event. I felt every emotion. Every feeling. I felt everything, but I did not feel through my perspective. I felt it through everyone's and everything's.

Not only was I living through all people with whom I had ever had contact, I was seeing myself through the plants, the earth and the water.

The alien being was correct. The trees surrounded me constantly. It was their eyes. I was seeing through them now. My heart sank.

They did not look at me with hostility. The ocean did not seek vengeance upon me for casting poison in its water. The ocean and the land looked at me with understanding and forgiveness. The same forgiveness I could not help but have when looking through the eyes of others. Others who had caused me pain.

Hatred at the wrong doings and suffering that others had inflicted upon me vanished. Hatred that had pushed me to wish death upon others vanished. I now understood them as I saw through their eyes. I saw through the eyes of us all. I saw through the eyes of the spirit we are all a part of and I could only have understanding and forgiveness, forgiveness not only for others but forgiveness for myself.

I watched as every night I would lie down to sleep and exit my physical body, entering a world of dreams. I watched as I created my own reality while my physical body slept and I watched as I created my own physical reality when I was awake. I watched through to my boyhood, cutting the tongue and cheek from the heads of codfish in the factories along the Norwegian coast. I watched until I was but a developing baby in my mother's womb.

I stared into my mother's womb. I stared at myself; the tiny creature that I was. A part of my mother, attached, inside her. Then suddenly my hands felt wet.

My hands were sinking into the pool. What was a solid was now liquefying, and I was sinking into it. My hands were submerging. I could not stop looking into the pool. My entire forearms quickly vanished and I could not stop from falling in. I had no sense of having any arms at all as they vanished completely. My forehead dipped and touched the liquid, my entire head submerged, and into the liquid crystal I fell.

Motionless, suspended and for a moment I felt I was in the womb surrounded by what felt like a mother, in a liquid that felt like home.

Yet I was falling down, slowly down, drifting through the veins of this alien world. My mind began to shift and I could not properly remember where I was. I could not properly remember what I was. I could not piece together any thoughts of my own, my mind become emptier and emptier as I drifted further.

Up and down had no meaning anymore, before or after and this or that melted into an incomprehensible soup as I drifted further along the veins of this alien world, not sure if I was anything at all. I drifted further away from myself until all I could vaguely remember was that I was some form of creature and that I lived on a large rock and that there was a sun. Then that was gone and all understanding of what I was and where I was from was gone. There was nothing. Blank.

Plonk!

I fell too.

I fell from the other end of the long liquid river, disorientated and I could not see, and I sat on what felt like wet ground. Time seemed to be as distant as any recollection of anything and I wasn't sure if I had arrived but a moment ago or if I had been there for an indefinite period.

I seemed to become familiar with where I was. Where I was seemed to become familiar and slowly my memory made light of itself.

I remembered going to the alien planet.

I remembered seeing my life in the pool, and I remembered falling in. Then I heard the same woman's voice, only this time it was not soft and it was not gentle. This time her voice was strong. Her voice was firm, yet in a strange way casual as if I was sitting in her kitchen. Her voice filled me and her voice was all that there was.

'Do you need to come all the way here to learn such simple things?'

She spoke harshly as if she was scolding me, as if I had disrupted her.

My eyes were closed so incredibly tight and it was an effort to open them, as if I had been asleep for a very long time. Slowly they opened, and I saw a small woman standing before me.

She had dark skin and long messy hair. She was not beautiful. Her skin looked damaged and what teeth she had were rotten. She reached her hands out to me, black filth covered them and the filth stretched up above her forearms as though she had been cleaning something dreadful. The stench from her hands consumed me and I struggled to focus.

The woman looked tired. Her feet were hard and callused as were her knees, she looked as though she had been working her skin to the bone with no time to rest. Her eyes were black, whole black and looking into them was like looking into an endless tunnel. She stared hard and she did not blink.

I froze.

I stared back.

I stared back in fear of looking away.

I stared in fear of what might happen if I did.

She pressed one of her large fingers to my forehead and I felt it. It felt real. Incredibly physical. I felt the layer of skin between her finger and my skull compress. I felt that if she kept pushing she would break my skull. Such strength moved in this woman and although her hands were stained black and deadly strong, they were soft and her touch felt nice, and her eyes, although black and piercing had a strange calming effect.

'Watching your reflection was not enough'

'You had to jump in,' the old woman said.

She stared at me and I thought her eyes might break me into pieces.

'No,' I said.

'I did not jump in. I fell.'

'I didn't even mean to come down here.'

She stared straight at me, still not blinking.

'You need this,' the old woman said as she plunged a large sword into the ground beside me. Then she pointed to a dark area in the distance.

I looked where she was pointing. It was dark, darker than I thought darkness could be and the feel of it brought a shudder. There was something there. There was something dark there. Something scary was there. Something scarier than any human could be.

It scared me.

It really scared me.

I felt it could not only take and eat my physical body but it could take and eat this one too. Fear ran through me, stabbing my throat.

Whatever was there, it was something I knew nothing about. It was an evil I had not met before, an evil that would feed me and fatten me before killing me.

Slap!

The old woman slapped me, hard. She slapped me within an inch of my passing out and going black. 'Look at where you are!' she demanded. Her words were so forceful I obeyed instantly.

I looked at where I was.

I was not inside any planet. I was somewhere different.

'You certainly are inside the planet,' the old woman said. Her focus fixed steadily. She had a plan. I felt she had a plan.

'You are within the crystalline that flows through this world and you did not fall in, you jumped!'

The old woman smiled, showing a face of irregular decayed teeth. 'You jumped into my pool,' she said, 'just as you threw down that cocaine you were handed on the streets of Lima. You don't see what parts of yourself are doing. But here it is different,' she said. 'Here you will see more.'

'This crystalline body of yours has entered my pool and the rest of you remains as it was, peering into it with your hands pressed against its hard surface. 'You want to fly your own spaceship? You can start with realising when you are jumping into something and when you are throwing something down.' I stared at the old woman; her black unblinking eyes, fearsome, yet warm and she carried a knowledge.

I looked around at where I was. Space, stars and planets. In every direction stars scattered the sky, and this light, this crystal liquid, solid beams of this light were running through all of them. Littering the sky, scattered in every direction as far as I could see were stars.

The old woman pushed the sword towards me, her voice slightly softer as she spoke, yet croaky in a splitting sort of way. She leaned forward toward me, her eyes reaching into the depths of me. He croaky voice sounded as though it might crack the very fabric that held me together.

'You cannot see the planet because it is not here and you cannot see your physical body because it is not here, both you and the planet exist on the heavier plains of the material dimensions.'

'Here you are perceiving through an even lighter body.'

The old woman stared.

'A body that connects this world to the stars.' She pointed up.

A beam of energy ran through this translucent planet and up connecting with a group of stars in the distance. In every direction beams of energy ran through this world and connected to both close and distant stars. In every direction stars connected to stars, to this world and each other. A spider web. A web of energy. I looked in every direction. A complex web of connections; connections forming multifaceted geometrical designs. A three-dimensional web of lines of connection, the same detailed designs I had seem within myself. A kaleidoscope of movement.

This formation was the same kaleidoscope that moved within the stone. It was the same formation that moved within me. It was the same formation that was running through me to others. The old woman pointed down and I looked at the huge beam of energy flowing from this world towards a distant spiralling galaxy.

'Your earth is home to this galaxy,' the old woman said. I looked down at the spiralling galaxy. I looked around at the many others. The old woman remained focused on me. 'Your galaxy and ours are becoming a part of the same system. We are moving closer together. We are becoming a part of the same formation as more connections are being joined through our worlds. The energy that flows through us will pass through your world.

'As your earth's inner structure changes, becoming a part of this new system, so too will the beings that walk the surfaces inner structure change. Change is coming to your world, and your earth will, in time, be harmonious. In time, all beings will live in harmony with themselves and with each other. There will come a time when all forms of your mental and emotional pain, along with your physical pains of war and struggle will be nothing but a story in your history books, never to be repeated again.'

'You will understand the nature of the universe and you will know the beings that you are and like many others you will consciously create the world that you wish to have. You will learn that consciousness is the creator and that you yourselves are the God that people of your time are now praying to.'

The woman rested one finger on the handle of the sword, which balanced into the crystalline.

'However,' she said. 'This will be a time of change and with all change, as with all transformation, there is loss. Loss of the old.'

'People will no longer wish to carry negativity. They will feel the poison that it is and free themselves from it. Your society will transform.'

The old woman's eyes had not moved from mine.

She pointed her large finger at a small space away from my chest.

'You believed you fell into this pool,' she said.

'You did not.'

'You jumped.'

'You made the decision to enter. A part of you made this decision. A part of yourself you are unaware of as you sleep in your physical body. It is the part of yourself that you must know in order to fly your own spaceship.'

She pushed the sword towards me, its handle falling into my palm.

It was the same sword.

It was the same sword I had taken from the statue in my dream and wished to push through the neck of the king.

It was light and it felt good to hold.

It felt like an extension of my arm and I felt somewhere I had carried such a sword before.

It was made from crystal and within its multifaceted sides it reflected a piece of myself.

I looked into the sword.

I looked at my own reflection - but it was not just me.

It was not just the 'me' here and now of this life.

It was all of them.

Every edge of crystal upon this sword reflected a life I had lived, a face staring back at me - thousands of them.

Every life I had ever lived, a face staring back at me.

The old woman's black unblinking eyes remained fixed in mine.

'This sword is you,' she said.

'You will take it and you will use it to cut the heavy energy that you are holding, the darker energies that still pass through your world. This sword lives inside you. Through it you will cut with your actions and your deeds. Using the instrument of your human form, you will cut these heavy energies away from yourself.'

She pointed to the dark area.

I looked, and cold sharp shivers ran the length of my spine. I froze stiff as I looked. The beings there were more than a mere threat of danger. I felt them. They were hungry. They were searching for food.

'I will clean now,' the old woman said.

'I will clean this poison. I will give light to this darkness so it may not pass itself to others and spread. So these beings may leave the torment of their own poison.'

'And you.'

'You,' she said. 'You will go back to your world and choose the path you will walk.'

I stared at this eerie poison, it was pushing for connection with this world, it was searching for life, it was searching for a home. It was searching for recognition and validation of its world, waiting for any being to enter. Waiting for its chance to draw the life force from them. It was unforgiving.

The old woman was fast.

She was fast and she was precise.

She took the sword from my hands and turned it with the blade down, quicker than my mind could follow she stood up and plunged the crystal sword through the top of my head. Pushing it hard through every disk of my spine!

Electricity!

Shock!

Every life I had ever lived, every life upon our earth ran through me and I saw all of them. I saw all of them at once.

Every life imaginable, from every country and every colour of skin.

Electricity, and as fast as I had seen each one of my selves, the electricity stopped, and I was back.

I was back in the spiral shaped building looking into the pool. Back with my hands on the solid crystal surface, looking at my reflection. Me, the ordinary reflection of me.

27. Return

I pushed myself away from the pool, and stood up staring at it. The hard crystal pool reflecting the usual me. The three alien beings stood beside me. Victoria stood in the centre of the room —and she had wings.

Victoria was glowing and she opened her eyes. A shine surrounded her. It was as if she was visiting from another world and was bringing that world with her. Calm and strong, a shine stitched into herself. Stitched into the fabric of the world we walked in. She stood glowing with crystal wings on her back.

The five of us walked.

We exited the building through another opening that led to a large courtyard and I looked around. The tall trees were towering over and there were many interestingly shaped buildings there. Soft ground with manicured stone lined the path that snaked through the courtyard and there were many beings gathered talking amongst themselves.

They stood and sat with each other, unconcerned with our presence as if foreigners such as us were common occurrence. They were exceptionally human like with the same structure that is our human form and, apart from their extreme difference in height, they were obviously the same species. All slim and elastic with long slender fingers and huge eyes. They sat and stood in groups, highly engaged in what ever it was they were talking about. All of them were naked.

The taller of the alien beings turned to me.

'I too have worn clothes,' he said. 'I have walked many worlds and I have worn clothes for decoration and for warmth. A long time ago I lived on a world where we all wore clothes.'

It seemed this being was making conversation, as if he merely wanted to chat; yet I felt he had a point he wished to make. I felt he had a reason for making this point. I felt time somehow had slipped away. I felt I had slipped away from the time I was in. I felt that he had already made his point and that the beginning of this conversation and the end of it were somehow in the same place. Then I felt the gentle breeze of the trees inside, their leaves brushing smoothly. I felt their roots hold deep and strong.

The alien being looked at me, smiling and I felt the trees holding us together as he told me of a world he once lived.

'For many reasons we wore clothes', he said. 'For protection from the weather of our world and to present ourselves to others in ways we otherwise could not. We all lived solidly in the mind of the individual and each of our own selves was the only being we could properly recognise.'

'To us—our world and each other, were a resource, something that was at our disposal. We claimed the earth as something that belonged to us. We claimed the minerals in the ground and we claimed the trees in the forest, and we claimed each other. In time our water became unfit to drink and the ground became unfit for plants to grow. We threw poison in the air and eradicated other species of the surface.

'We ate each other and it was normal.'

'We were separate from each other, so much so, we were feeding off each other and not only were we feeding on the physical bodies of each other, we were feeding on others energy. We had lost contact with ourselves, with the parts of ourselves that are connected to each other and these parts of ourselves were crying out for food. We did not understand it was our inner self that was crying for us to come back to it. To come back and feel the sustenance that is the sharing of energy between each other. We did not understand how to share the unlimited energy that we are a part of and we tried to bring forcefully such sustenance into our lives. Constantly we sought for this energy from others, through their attention towards us, through their fear of us and admiration of us.'

'We were lost in a constant search for food for our inner self, and our accumulation of what we considered wealth to be and our dominance over others only brought temporary illusion, never the food we sought. Our priorities were wrong for what we were trying to achieve, and we experienced sensations that do not exist on this planet. Such sensations as pain, fear and misery. Lost in a quest of ownership of our world, the things we owned were actually owning us. Never did we find the sustenance we sought in this way, we only found lessons.'

'There were beings on our surface who believed they owned our entire world. They believed they were not only rulers of sections of the surface, but all of it. These beings did not hear themselves. To our race, the trees were wood and others were slaves and it did not matter what we left for our children, because we were not the children.'

'Our earth supported us through this period of growth. It supported us physically and was speaking to us always, even though we did not hear her.'

The thin being held up his hand extending a long slender finger and paused.

'I have been to many worlds', he said. 'I have been to worlds made of matter much heavier than your earthly plains. Worlds where singing and dancing does not exist. Worlds where beauty is unrecognisable. I have been to worlds where every moment is a fight, where every being lives in darkness and where every being is but food for another.'

'Some worlds do not know mercy.'

The alien paused. He paused yet I felt there was more. I flashed back to my dream, standing by the doors of the school that sat on the mountains—the old man said he could not tell what the school would be like for me—he could only say what it was like for him.

I flashed back to the old woman in the crystal pool—she said we were the gods that we were praying to—she said we were the creator.

I stared at the alien being and I wondered what it was to look through his eyes. I looked at Victoria and again I wondered what it was that she was hearing.

Buildings of complex description lined the courtyard and a small one caught my eye, as if it were hidden yet it stood out in a different sort of way. I looked at the small intricately decorated doorway leading to the small building, a door carved from the rock.

'Birth and death is a conscious decision here,' the alien said pointing to the small building, 'and when it is right for one to take form, they will walk from the doorway of stone and enter this world.'

He looked at me, and pointed to the courtyard. 'Every building contains a pool,' he said, 'however some pools you will not see unless you look very close, and sometimes' the alien being said, 'to see such pools you must look through eyes which are closed.' I stared at this being and wondered how it could be that one could look through eyes that were not open. The alien being just smiled and continued speaking.

'Pools of different material are the body of, and the home to, different beings. Old and wise beings that hold connection between planets and stars. As you enter these pools, you enter parts of yourself that you do not usually hear or see. It is with the guidance of such beings that dwell within them that we learn how to use these parts of ourselves. We learn how to work with the materials of metals and stone that lie beneath the surface. Such materials are used to build the spacecraft that is able to move through both time, and the different vibrational worlds that sit on top of each other.'

'There are ships bigger than your earth,' the alien being said.

The smallest of the three walked through the huge stone courtyard and we followed.

We followed along a stone path lined with the tremendous trees that covered this world. We walked until we came to a very big clearing. A clearing with large stones lining the ground that fit snugly together. Stone that looked like skin, stone that fit snugly and beautifully together, like the skin of a chameleon.

The clearing was huge and I could barely see the other side. Towering trees surrounded the clearing and spacecraft were everywhere. There was spacecraft bigger than our biggest cities and there was spacecraft small enough for one or two.

We walked and stood in front of what seemed to be the smallest. It was translucent. I could see right through it and it looked light, as if I could pick it up and hurl it to any destination. Yet it looked heavy, as if it could sink into the very ground it stood on.

I looked at the huge ship off in the distance. It was astronomically huge, thousands of storeys high. It was not translucent and looked to be made of a strange material. The small alien being pointed to the large ship. 'It is much bigger from the inside,' he said.

'This world and these ships can be much bigger from the inside, for such material is alive and it is not only that you enter the spacecraft, not only do you enter such pools that run through this world but you are entering a different world where space and time cannot only be different, it can entirely not exist.' I stared at the huge ship.

'It is large enough for your entire galaxy to fit within,' the alien being said.

The small translucent ship was spherical. A round disk with an area inside to situate oneself. 'Crystal,' the alien said, 'this ship is made from the crystal pool you both entered and no force other than itself can penetrate it. This is the ship you will take back to your world. You both carry inside of yourself a part of this being, and it is not you who will fly this ship. It is her.'

'Only those who are connected with her will be able to see this ship.'

The tallest of the three turned to both Victoria and I.

'Use the sword that lies within you to cut free the darkness that runs through your world. With every interaction you have cut free the dark energy and let open channels of light.' The being fixed his eyes solely on me. 'Dark energy cannot flow through this crystal, for dark energy cannot see, feel or hear on such a frequency. If you do not cut the dark energy containing fear and hate with that sword, you will drop it. You will drop it and you will not even realise you have. You will drop it and you will not remember having it at all.'

The being turned his eyes from mine to Victoria.

'Continue to use your wings as you have been. Helping to pick people up and carry them away from darkness and into the light.'

Victoria walked through the transparent craft and stood in its centre. I watched as she crystallised and became a part of it, as transparent as the craft surrounding her. I looked at the three alien beings, their huge eyes and their thin elastic body's. I listened, waiting for them to speak, but it was not them who spoke. Again it was the trees.

Such powerful laughter moved with their words. 'We are always with you,' they said, 'our branches are always out and our roots are always deep.'

The trees were speaking through their laughter, the same laughter I had heard in the Amazon. I looked at the tall trees and to the three beings standing before me, and then walked into the centre of the spacecraft, joining Victoria.

I entered and standing before us was the same woman. Yet she was beautiful. Her skin was glowing and her eyes shone striking colours of blue, brown and green. She was the most beautiful woman I had ever seen. A long silky dress fell easily over the contours of her body and surrounding her was a glow. A glowing white light that filled the craft. It was so bright I could see nothing else. A soothing light ran through me. It was soothing and strong. Everything of this alien world was gone, as we become a part of the energy that dwelled within her.

Not me, not Victoria not the craft. Nothing but light and the same soft whispering voice of this gentle woman.

'You will fly your own ship,' she said, 'but now I will take you back to your world, for it is your world where you must be. It is your world where you must learn to use the sword that lies within you and fly with the wings that you are a part of. It is your world, through your human form that allows you the circumstances that you require to proceed with the transformation to a new form.'

'To a new world,' she said. 'A new you that allows your dreams to really come true.'

28. Back to our old world

It was as if we had never left.

Time—such an occurrence.

Looking down through the transparent walls of the spacecraft at our blue and green planet, I watched the earth turn. I watched as the sunlight moved across the earth, coming to wake the Americas, peeling its way across the Atlantic bringing morning to the long landmass that stretched through one hemisphere to the other.

We headed down toward the mountain ranges of the Andes. It was quite a sight from this perspective, running through the centre of the continent separating the Amazon jungle from the coast. We headed down to the meditation centre and landed in the grassy clearing between the hall and the fruit trees.

I stood looking out through the transparent walls of the craft. I watched as the doors of the meditation hall opened and all who had been sitting walked out. They walked slowly, dressed in their warm clothes to the dining hall. No one noticed us. None noticed that we were there standing in the centre of a spacecraft that sat right beside them.

No one noticed except the meditation teacher who stood looking directly at us. She did not smile, nor did she frown, she just stood looking. I looked back at her. She stood as strong and composed as a statue. I looked at her and I wondered.

29. Living the new reality

I opened my eyes.

I could feel the bones in my body. I could feel the flesh around my bones. I could feel the skin around my flesh. I felt exceptionally physical. Cool air ran over the bumps of my skin, brushing the hairs on my arms into each other.

I felt fresh and elastic, with not a pinch of stiffness as I leaned forward and stretched my arms out in front of me. Lying with my cheek on the cool floor, I looked in Victoria's direction; she sat still and upright, her hands resting in her lap.

I felt strong and pushing myself away from the floor and up to my feet was effortless. Walking was effortless. I pushed the door open and walked outside. I walked slowly and I looked carefully. I could see everything. Absolutely everything. Every blade of grass, I could see the tiny details of the fibres that covered them. I could feel in a way I had never felt before. With every step I could feel the pressure of myself on the ground. I could feel the fibres of muscle move as I stepped. I could feel every blade of grass crease under my footsteps.

I could see everything. I felt like radar. The veins that ran along each leaf of the trees that lined the garden, every vein of every leaf, every leaf on every tree and every flower that was underneath them. Each petal of each flower. Such vibrant colours. Such detail. All of them. All of them at the same time. I saw every detail of them all. I heard the wind that pushed past every one of them, brushing them into one another. I could hear each individual leaf and I could hear the sounds of all the trees rustling together.

I walked from the meditation hall to the dinning room.

Again it was porridge for breakfast.

I took a cup of tea and found a quiet place in the sun and lay down. The grass was soft and the earth was cold, the sun shining on my face was warm, and I lay soaking in it. I felt the same life I had felt on the alien world. The life in our world. The beings that live behind the curtains were here. The beings of the mountains. The beings of the trees and the beings of the earth. They were here. I closed my eyes feeling the sun heat my eyelids, thinking about the sword the old woman had plunged inside me. I thought how her hands and teeth were dirty. How tired she looked. I thought how I saw her again and she was clean and beautiful.

'They must have seen something special in you, that you may enter such a pool.'

I opened my eyes to see the meditation teacher standing over me.

I sat up and she sat down.

I looked at her. I didn't quite know what to say. She obviously knew these worlds and she had seen us when we landed.

'They did not see anything special in me,' I said. 'I learnt we are all a part of the same. I am no more special than any other. We are all working together as one living being.' I looked at her and she looked at me. 'Well,' she said, as if I had answered her question, 'that is what they saw.'

'You were not given this sword, Alexander,' the meditation teacher said. 'You were simply shown that you already had it and you can never loose it. You can only forget that you have it. There is much for you to discover about yourself and the power that lies within us. The magic we hold within us is limited by nothing.'

'We must treat all as a brother and sister to connect with these worlds. To connect with the parts of ourselves that are dwelling in such worlds. To connect with the parts of ourselves which are the same parts as others selves. We must give ourselves fully to others or we will remain separate from them and our self. We must treat all as a brother and sister.'

The meditation teacher smiled.

'However you are here, in this world,' she said. You are your physical human self here, and the interactions you have with others are but situations. Situations at your request, situations that allow you to become that which you wish to become. To learn what is necessary. To share what is necessary.'

I looked at her.

'To learn what?' I asked.

'To learn love,' she said, 'and to give others the necessary situations so that they may learn love.' To find yourself and to create yourself.'

The meditation teacher smiled, it was a smile I could not read. I could not read all of it, but it was nice.

I looked around the garden. Never before had I felt so much for the trees and plants. An interaction with the spiritual world. What beings these plants were, the trees, the grass, and the flowers, how these beings gave to us, so vulnerable. Giving us air to breathe, food to eat and such displays of beauty. The healing powers they had for our wounds, both physical and in the case of the night I spent with Pi in the jungle, mental and spiritual healings too.

'Yes,' said the teacher.

'Yes,' and she placed her hand on mine. 'The spiritual is, as is the body you travelled in these past days, you interacting with yourself. Yourself presenting yourself with situations you wish for, for your learning. She leaned forward and whispered in my ear.

'Love this world,' she said. 'Show love to every other and you will connect with love. You will connect with it and it will fill you, you will swim in it. It will be a part of you and you will live with it always. Become a connection of love and you will not only attain everlasting happiness but you will be able to share in such happiness with others. You will enter the world that it lives in—worlds that are real'

She smiled and looked as though she might break into a chuckle. It was a smile that understood that she knew I had not grasped all of what she was speaking.

The little bell sounded and the old teacher rose easily from the ground. She walked across the garden to the hall as though a cloud were carrying her. I watched her, and I wondered what other doors lay hidden of this world. I smiled as I watched the others from the dining hall follow.

The hall was quiet.

The room was still and as people shuffled finding positions of comfort, I felt my body slip away.

I was no longer surprised by the oddities or the accuracies that took place; they were merely as odd as the oddities I had lived with, so comfortably familiar with for the many years I had lived. The many years I had been at sea taking fish from the ocean. The many years I had been walking the surface of this earth in my peculiar form. A form that is equally peculiar as the being that was now walking happily through the centre of the room.

He was green and he reminded me slightly of the beings that I had only just visited. He was slim and he was short, much shorter than me and his big eyes and large pointy ears made his appearance to be that of an elf like creature. His fingers were long and slender like the alien beings and his naked body looked muscular yet soft and elastic. He walked in a most peculiar way as though he was making fun of the way he was walking.

It was an extraordinary sight, as he walked making fun of the way he was walking, he was making a very merry and extraordinarily happy tune. He was walking to the tune he was making.

I was struck, compelled by the presence of this creature, who did not look in my direction. He just continued to walk through the room, unconcerned that my eyes following him as he moved to his own music. His music filled the room. He was dancing to his own tune. He was making fun of his own dancing. His music filled me. A remarkable melody. A tune that could be described as powerfully funny and merry.

 Leaves and small brightly coloured flowers were growing and falling from this being and resting on the floor leaving a trail of colour in his path and as he walked past me, my eyes followed him, and, as my eyes followed him—his music seemed to follow me. His music grew stronger.

I couldn't make out if the music was soft or loud. I could not quite distinguish between the music and myself. I could not quite distinguish where I began and where the music stopped. I could not quite distinguish if I was myself listening to the music or if I were the music playing to myself.

A world of sound.

A world, as alive as I am.

Sound, as alive as I am.

All beings that were within me, all the cells within me were sound. Sounds all playing themselves. I was them, my own sound, my own rhythm, my own symphony. The music played and I felt the vastness of what this being was. He did not turn or look in my direction yet I heard him as he passed; happily continuing on his walk with the business he was attending to. A quick pass and not even a look my way, yet I heard him as he spoke through the sound that filled the room. His music reached into me and pulled power into my being, it shook a swell in my eyes.

'I live with you and we are the spirits of the earth and here is where we live. We are who we wish to be. We love who we are and we wish for you to be the same. We feed you and hold you as you grow. We are the ground you walk on and the food you eat. We are the fairies in the trees and the elves in the forest. We are the dragons in the mountains.'

'I am whatever physical body I choose and I live with the physical world.'

'I am whatever spiritual body I choose and I live with the spiritual world.'

'I am what you see before you. I am my own creation of my own song. I am in physical and in spirit, my own image. I am my own animation.'

'I am my imagination.'

With that he passed through the walls of the building and was out of sight. The music stopped and he was gone.

30. Joy

Voices filled the dining hall. Some talked eagerly after being deprived of speech for so many days and some were quiet, adjusting back to the world they had left. Day ten, and silence was over.

I took a piece of fruit and a bowl of vegetables and sat outside. I sat with the sun on my face looking at the food in my bowl and for the first time ever I said a prayer before I ate. For the first time ever I had reason to.

I ate slowly.

The process of eating.

I picked a piece of vegetable from the bowl. I could see where the blade had cut through it. Directly connected to the spirit that it is a part of. I was having a physical interaction and I was having an interaction that was a communion far from physical. I was sharing in the energy and the vibration of this being's physical element. It was not only feeding me physically, it was feeding me in spirit, sharing its vibration and sharing its frequency. A vibration so subtle I had never heard it before over the incredible noise that was my life.

I looked at the pear in my hand and chuckled. I laughed at the giving of thanks before eating. When the thanks I felt now went hand in hand with the interaction being made and what was being shared.

The outside of the pear had become warm with the sun but the inside was still cool from the morning chill. How much I could taste when I tasted. How much I could feel when I felt and how much you could hear when listening. I wished for all to taste this fruit, for all who had never tasted such a pear to taste this fruit. For all who had never really tasted to eat and to share with such beings.

I looked around the garden. I looked at what had always been there. A spider on a huge web right where we had all been passing many times a day. I watched a street dog walk casually through the grounds. I watched an insect as it hopped in the grass and as another meditator walked past the dog, they both turned and looked at each other.

Our world, I thought, is just like the beings I had met, whose form was new and completely different in concept from that with which I was familiar. How we are as they are. Such a combination of all that we have been evolving through, such an equally uncanny display of physical form. How comfortable we are within the walls of such a bizarrely obscure, yet totally normal surrounding.

Fishing.

I took my phone from my pocket and looked at the date. I was due back to the coast of Norway in a few days.

I had not climbed a mountain and I had not been to the Ruins of Machu Picchu. However I had climbed a different mountain and I had been to other ruins. Ruins and mountains that were inside myself.

I lay in the grass feeling the sun.

Feeling comfortable.

Incredibly comfortable.

31. Landing

Spain.

I listened to the flight crew describe the weather and our landing time as we began to descend. I looked at my travel itinerary as the wheels of the plane hit the runway, skidding and bouncing until we were smoothly on the ground. I leaned over Victoria looking through the window at the large airport tarmac of Madrid. I looked at the pink and green hyper colour travel case decorated with small fairies that lay in her lap. I thought it was good we had left the cheque for two thousand dollars with the meditation centre.

Victoria stirred, opening her eyes as the plane turned and pulled into the gate. The seatbelt sign turned off and it was the usual rush that came with the landing of the plane, as all who could hurriedly squeezed into the aisle and reached for their bags.

Flying reminded me of fishing.

Flying to and from port where the ship docked. It reminded me of two things, heading to the ship and leaving it. Now I was on my way there, back to the darkness of the winter. Back to spending my days dressed in weather gear. Back to spending my days killing fish.

We sat watching the passengers push from their seats to the aisle and stand crowded, waiting for the plane doors to open. We watched as the doors opened and the flood of people pushed their way through. Victoria moved her eyes from the movement of people to me. 'As if this is the only way to travel,' she said.

I looked at her. She was searching my eyes. She was searching for a response, staring into me like she was looking at a fish tank of movement within, waiting to see which part of me would respond.

Waiting to see how she could proceed with the information she wished to share.

The plane became emptier as the remaining passengers stood and collected their bags from the overhead. I stood up and reached for my things, looking at Victoria, waiting for her to elaborate on another means of transport from South America to Scandinavia. Victoria smiled. It was a smile I recognised, the same smile I had seen on the meditation teacher. 'You are your thoughts,' she said.

'We are living in our own dream holding our self together with our own thoughts. Deep within the being of yourself you are holding your physical form together. Know yourself. Know the parts of yourself that are holding the physical being that you walk in together and you will be able to disassemble and reassemble yourself into any form you wish. You will be able to move through the lighter worlds and you will no longer need to fly in this big heavy aircraft.'

I looked at Victoria. We were the last remaining passengers and the flight crew was packing their things, and were doing a sweep of the plane. We walked off the aircraft and through the boarding gate.

I looked at my boarding card at my connecting flight to Oslo. I needed to go.

I looked at Victoria.

'I have to go,' I said.

Victoria searched my eyes, looking for something.

She pulled the threaded necklace from under my shirt and let it hang on the outside. She turned a few of the seeds over between her fingers then looked up at me smiling.

'I'll see you,' she said.

I looked at the necklace and I looked to her. I stood with her until my name was called over the intercom.

Back to the Norwegian coast.

The Secret Window

32. Aha!

I closed the door of the taxi and looked towards the ship. Pallets of bait lined the dock and were being hoisted to the ship and lowered to the freezer.

I walked aboard and threw my bag to the room that was always mine.

The ship carried that same smell. That smell you only realise is hanging to the walls of the ship when you have been away from it. The smell of fish and the smell of a factory that has had countless fish pass through it. The smell would soon pass, unnoticed, as my nose would become adjusted. It always becomes adjusted to the smell.

I walked from my room towards the mess, when a young man looking no older than fresh from school turned the corner in a hurry. He was not looking where he was going and walked right into me. He lost his balance and would have fallen if the thin passage of the ship hadn't caught him.

'You alright?' I asked.

He looked up, 'Yes,' he said.

His frame was thin and his head was large. Huge front teeth stuck out of his mouth as if his head had not caught up with them. He forced an unnatural smile as he spoke. 'Sorry,' he said.

I knew him. I knew him from somewhere. He was familiar.

'You lost?' I asked.

'No,' he replied, 'Dimitri told me to open the back hatches and drop the food to the kitchen.'

I stared at him. Dimitri was back on the ship. I stared and I wondered how Dimitri was. I wondered how his face looked now. I wondered how he expected this new boy to open the hatches alone.

'Come,' I said, 'I will help you.'

I turned on the hydraulics and started up the crane, and threw a sling to the dock where several pallets of food waited to be lifted aboard. We unscrewed the wing nuts securing the hatch and fastened the crane to it. I lifted up the large steel hatch exposing the topside of the pantry where the food was to be stored.

The new boy was clumsy, yet he was unconcerned with his clumsiness or the forced smile that never went away. He did not know where to be or what to do and as I looked at him trying to pinpoint where I had seen him before, he looked at me for direction. He was keen to help, and I thought to myself—such a forced smile this boy carried.

'The food,' I said.

I lowered the wire of the crane over a pallet of food that lay on the dock. 'Come,' I said, 'I will show you how to fix it.' We walked to the dock and as I was showing him how to fix the sling around the pallet of food, Russ arrived.

I leaned on the pallet of food and watched as Russ exited the taxi. He walked towards me, a smile stretched across his face, and as I waited to greet him, Dimitri's voice came calling down from the deck of the ship.

I looked up at Dimitri.

His face did not look bad and I was relieved to see he was alive and functioning with no disfigurement.

'Good to see you are alive,' I called out.

Dimitri leaned over the balustrade of the ship. 'It is good to see you are also alive Alexander,' he said. He did not smile and as I looked closer at his face, I saw his eyes were a little black and his nose sat on an awkward angle. He pointed at the food.

'Tie it on,' he said, 'we are here to work. I looked at him, and then I looked at Russ who stood leaning against the pallet of food, a smile pushing his cheeks to his eyes.

Nothing had changed. The ship was the same. It was life as usual. I looked at the pallets of food lining the dock. The same food was ordered, the same food that has always been ordered. Dimitri was the same and Russ was the same and as usual there was a new member to the crew, fresh from school. I looked to the bridge as the skipper stepped from inside the wheelhouse to the outside deck, waving casually at us. He talked on the phone, the same calm usual self that he was.

We brought up the pallets of food and lowered them to the pantry. Everything was the same. We brought on ice, bait and oil as we always did and we let the lines go and moved away from the dock. We stored the lines inside away from the ice winter and headed north to our fishing ground.

The crew sat in the mess drinking coffee. The news played on the TV and the cook was preparing the same recipe of pork and potatoes he made every week. I wasn't hungry. The smell of tobacco moved through the mess, as did the pork roasting in the oven. I leaned into the sofa and closed my eyes.

There was no silence here. This was no meditation centre. The television was always on and the news reporters always spoke in the same robotic tones as they spoke of tragedy and of sporting events. To them, to most everyone else, and to the ship, the ocean is a resource. Fish are meat and trees are wood and the left overs from the products we produce, is rubbish. Rubbish to be discarded, and in this case discarded to the sea.

The cook took the pork roast from the oven and sliced it, then placed it on the warming tray. Animals that we eat. We raise them and feed off them. Animals who are a part of the same life force as ourselves, animals who eat the plants. Plants who feed off light.

I was now where Vegor had been. I did not wish to kill fish; I did not wish to kill anything. I did not wish to throw garbage to the sea and I did not wish to eat the meat the cook had just laid on the table. I had asked for change and I had got it. Yet I was on a fishing boat and animals are served. Fish would be caught and the freezer would become full and rubbish would be thrown to the sea. The television in the mess would always play and the news reporters would always report the same news and they would report it in the same way.

This is the way things are.

Earth. Us. Humans.

The way we live on our earth. I could change. I could change and never again throw poison to the sea. I could never again kill another or eat the flesh of another. I could see that we are all a part of the same body, and I could never again inflict pain on another. But I was here, on this ship, on this earth and we were here to take fish. We were here to make money and everything is completely normal. I pushed myself up from the sofa and walked outside.

The snow was coming down. Light fluffy flakes fell slowly to the ocean and covered the deck of the ship. The ocean was calm and we moved through it at full speed leaving a visible wake behind us. I looked up at the falling snow. It fell into my eyes and melted as it touched my skin. I stepped over the garbage, which was the remains from unpacking food and bait and I found a spot to sit and looked out to the darkness of the ocean. Nothing but the sounds of the engine, and water hitting the sides of the ship. I sat watching and listening.

I listened to the sound of the hatch open. It was hurriedly closed again and light footsteps came up the metal steps to the deck where I sat. It was the thin new boy who was always smiling. He did not see me, and he grabbed a bag of garbage with both hands. I sat watching him, hidden in the dark, hidden with the snow that fell and the sounds of the churning propeller. He grabbed a bag, and struggling with it, he dragged it towards the side of the ship.

'You choose a funny time to clean up,' I said. He paused, looking for where my voice was coming from. He turned all the way around, even looking up and nearly tripping on his own feet. I reached out and touched him, giving him a shock that I was so very close. 'I have to clean the deck,' he said, as he wrestled with the garbage trying to lift it over the railing.

I stood up.

The heavy snow made visibility poor, yet I could see them clearly. They were standing right next to the boy. They were staring at me. Pi and his father. I stared at them, and they were not alone. The musical elf creature was with them, resting against the bulkhead, casually with his legs stretched out and his arms folded as if he was by a lone tree in an open field. Small flowers and leaves were falling from him and were taken with the wind, a stream of colour to be seen through the snow that trailed the ship. He did not look at me; he looked to the ocean, comfortably as if waiting for someone to arrive.

Both Pi and his father's faces were expressionless, as the boy continued to wrestle with the garbage, working it over the railing. I turned from them to the boy. I stared at him and he dropped the garbage and stood looking at me. 'We do not throw garbage to the sea from this ship,' I said.

The boy froze.

'They told me I had to,' he said. 'They told me if I didn't clean the deck by morning I would never keep a job here.'

I saw the light that ran through this boy, the same light that ran through us all and I saw something else. Connections with darkness. Connections with fear. Connections with fear that held him running to a task earlier that day he could not complete alone. Connections with fear that held him rushing to the outside deck when dinner was on and snow was falling. Connections with fear that held him easily manipulated by others, who fed off him through the same dark connections.

'There will always be someone willing for you to run for them and serve them,' I said, 'but this is not that ship and we do not serve each other here. We must work together and we must not work out of fear. We must work to attain a goal that is desirable for us all. I took the garbage the young boy was struggling with and threw it to the deck above the bridge. 'We store the garbage here,' I said. I grabbed another bag, and threw it through the heavy snow.

The boy dropped his smile. He dropped his smile and it was replaced with something else. Something calm. I stared at the boy.

He had given me an opportunity. To take his vulnerability and mould it into a shape I felt like having, or I could take his vulnerability and throw it to the ocean and share with him my strength. He looked different without that smile. He looked calm.

Pi and his father turned and the musical elf creature stood up and they all looked out toward the ocean. I let the bag of rubbish sit beside me and looked out to sea in the direction that Pi, his father and this green creature focused. The new boy looked at me as I set the bag of rubbish down, and again he tried to lift it.

The hatch opened and closed and the voice of the skipper spoke loud enough to be heard over the engine and the ocean, the boy stopped struggling with the garbage. The new boy's eyes were on the captain and the captain's eyes, along with Pi and his father's, were on me. The thin green plant spirit being still looked to the sea.

'What is this banging going on here?' the skipper asked. The skipper looked at me puzzled, worried that something was happening he would have to address. I took the bag of rubbish from the young boys hands and threw it to the top of the bridge, letting the skipper hear the thud that it made. 'It is better there than in the ocean,' I said to the skipper.

The captain, who was dressed with indoor slippers and a thin sweater, turned his collar up. 'Good,' he said, 'but go inside for heavens sake.' He waved his hand for us to leave the deck. 'It's snowing a blizzard our here, eat some food and rest,' he said, looking towards the new boy and before closing the hatch to the bridge he called through the snow. 'We have a lot of fishing ahead of us.'

The skipper closed the hatch and walked back inside and the young boy looked at me for permission to leave. Never again did he force a smile towards me, and as the new boy made for the mess I took another bag and threw it to the top of the bridge.

The green musical being took a step toward the railing of the ship, shifting his gaze as if he had just caught sight of what he was waiting for. Pi and his father moved their attention from me to where the green being was looking. I dropped the garbage I was holding when I felt the presence sweep through the ship.

It swept through the air.

It swept through everything. Through me, pushing me hard, a strong wind, a bad wind, strong like death. I froze. I had felt this before. This is what the old woman had been cleaning. Shock ran through me.

The green spirit, Pi and his father turned and faced me as this presence, this being, whatever it was moved around the deck of the ship.

Electricity ran down my spine.

The hairs on my neck stood up.

This presence.

It was not good.

It moved slowly around the deck—around me—an invisible predator. Moving slowly becoming familiar with its prey. It carried a frightening patience and moved around sniffing, contemplating how to take the life that is mine.

Patient as a crocodile, time meant nothing to it. Its strength, its frightening strength, as strong as it had to be to capture its prey, and merciless unconcerned with what pain it will inflict. Its eyes were on its prey. Its eyes were scratching to enter my mind.

It scared me.

It really scared me.

It was scratching at parts of myself I could barely touch, and it wanted to enter. I could not properly focus.

Overwhelmingly strong. It was circling me. This presence. Looking for an opportunity to reach into my mind. Looking to feed. Circling for what it could take, in search of not one meal but a lasting supply.

As it moved past Pi and his father they looked towards it and an expression of sadness filled their eyes.

It ignored them and moved to me, rushing with force.

It rushed quickly with force, yet at the same time it was slow and in a strange way it seemed gentle.

Gentle.

It was gentle.

Unbelievably gentle and then it spoke. It spoke and it was not as I had expected it to speak.

It spoke calmly and patiently.

'Power,' it said.

'I will give you power. All you could wish for upon this earth will be yours.'

'You will rule this land and have all you desire and all others will kneel before you.'

It was so very strong and I felt it spoke the truth, that it could deliver me wealth and status of the land.

'It cannot dwell in this world,' Pi said.

'It cannot even see you. It is not even aware of the form that you are. It is seeking for you to accept what offerings it has for you. It feels you and will offer you what ever it is that may capture you. It will not break its promise and will fulfil whatever you ask of it.'

'However, you will become absorbed in whatever it provides for you, as you indulge in whatever fantasies you have. You will willingly seek connection with it and it will then have gained control over you. It will break you away from every connection you have with others and the stars. You will have no power of your own and you will not look to others for a sharing of energy. You will look to it. You will no longer be able to feel the free flowing energy that moves between us and it will feed on you. It will feed on you and you will become a servant to a being that is stronger, and can dominate you in every way, for it will have control over your mind. You will continue to serve it and it will continue to feed on you until you let go of that which it can control you with.'

I felt the predator that was hunting retract deeper into the shadows as Pi spoke.

'This is the energy it is after,' Pi said. 'Our light. This part of us that carries everlasting life and unlimited potential. This is the energy it seeks yet it is too afraid to leave its world and share in it. Instead it seeks to bring others to its world and take what it can from them.'

Pi and his father stood on the deck and the green elf like creature again looked comfortable with his arms folded resting against the bulkhead. Leaves continued to fall from him and were taken with the wind, blowing a trail of colour behind the ship.

He began to hum.

This plant spirit being began a soft and very tantalizing tune.

'Spirits of this world are watching Alexander.'

'They are always watching and they are whispering to you. Spirits of this earth and spirits of others. They offer their hands and they offer their song and their hands are always out and their song is always playing.'

I looked from Pi and his father to the green spirit being, his tune was becoming louder and was spreading through more of the ship. I looked over the ocean. The force that sought me was now passing and moving across the sea.

It left.

Lightness came over me as it moved away, but it had left something behind. A part of it remained here. It had left an opportunity, an offer that always stood should I ever wish to accept it. I turned back from the sea to Pi, but he was gone. The green spirit being was also gone, but faintly I heard his melody. His melody seemed to creep from his world to ours, sliding through the cracks of an invisible door. I looked to where they stood and through the falling snow I threw the last bag of garbage to the deck above the bridge.

I went to leave the cold night, only to stop. I looked down at my feet. I did not shudder, nor did the hairs on my neck stand up. I looked down to see the most incredibly frightened creature I had seen.

It was tiny.

A tiny bird.

I had seen young birds on the ship before, but this bird was different.

It was a baby chick. Its new small grey feathers hardly covered its pink body that showed signs of being but a few moments old. It shook and quivered in the blistering cold. Its tiny beak opened and closed as it gasped for air, learning for the first time to use the instrument it is. Its small eyes were cloudy and it looked sick, as sick as poison.

It was alone, cold and scared. I knelt down and scooped it up. It shook, nestling itself close in my hands. I heard it. It was crying. It was crying and it was shaking. It was weeping, shaking and afraid. I looked at this helpless creature.

This powerful predator that had woken such vulnerability within myself was itself afraid, burring itself into my hands. I stared at its murky eyes. Full of poison. This creature was full of poison. It was seeing through poisonous eyes. The same eyes I had seen through before. The same poison I had lived with before. This creature wanted to be free from its poison as much as I had. I held the bird close in my hands protecting it from the weather. I wanted to take away its pain. I wanted to free it from its poison. I held it close.

Then something shifted inside.

Something shifted inside myself and something woke up.

Myself.

I stepped out of my self.

I stepped out of myself and I looked at myself.

I stood there staring.

Bald, with a long white beard, smiling, showing the same space between his front teeth that I had.

It was the old man from my dreams.

It was me. The old man from my dreams stood smiling

Such power he was connected to. There was no fear in his world. He could not be manipulated. Nothing could be taken from him. There was nothing he wanted and everything he had he wished to share.

The old man knelt down next to me. He placed the sword in front of him and knelt before it, pressing his forehead to the deck.

I was holding the shaking bird between my hands and the old man was knelt, his forehead pressed to the deck. He was surrendering himself. He was surrendering himself to the sword. He was giving himself to the cause for which the sword was fighting. He was obtaining the strength of the sword. He turned his head and he looked at me. I turned my head and I looked at him. We both looked in the same direction.

It had been there all along.

Right in front of my eyes.

It was open.

The secret window.

FIN